"Mars

His _____, _____ her fore-
arm, holding her in place. "No need. No real
harm done."

Slowly, his gaze traveled from her face downward, making her vividly aware that she was
wearing only a thin nightgown. The hand holding her gentled until his fingers stroked rather
than imprisoned. A heated gleam lit up his dark
eyes.

The moment she started to pull away, his
grip tightened again. One tug brought her
sprawling full-length on top of him.

"Marsh!"

That was all she got out before he covered
her mouth with his own.

This wasn't the time or the place for seduction, but he didn't stop kissing Linnea. He
couldn't. He'd have gone further if the faint
sound of someone calling her name hadn't penetrated the haze of rapidly building passion.

A single taste was not enough.

Soon—very soon—he and Linnea were going to finish what they had started.

WHAT ARE *LOVESWEPT* ROMANCES?

They are stories of true romance and touching emotion. We believe those two very important ingredients are constants in our highly sensual and very believable stories in the LOVE-SWEPT line. Our goal is to give you, the reader, stories of consistently high quality that may sometimes make you laugh, sometimes make you cry, but are always fresh and creative and contain many delightful surprises within their pages.

Most romance fans read an enormous number of books. Those they truly love, they keep. Others may be traded with friends and soon forgotten. We hope that each LOVESWEPT romance will be a treasure—a "keeper." We will always try to publish

LOVE STORIES YOU'LL NEVER FORGET
BY AUTHORS YOU'LL ALWAYS REMEMBER

The Editors

Loveswept ®
825

LOVE THY NEIGHBOR

KATHY LYNN EMERSON

BANTAM BOOKS
NEW YORK · TORONTO · LONDON · SYDNEY · AUCKLAND

LOVE THY NEIGHBOR

A Bantam Book / February 1997

*LOVESWEPT and the wave design are registered trademarks of
Bantam Books, a division of Bantam Doubleday Dell Publishing Group,
Inc. Registered in U.S. Patent and Trademark Office and elsewhere.*

ISBN 0-553-44572-3

Published simultaneously in the United States and Canada

*Bantam Books are published by Bantam Books, a division of Bantam Dou-
bleday Dell Publishing Group, Inc. Its trademark, consisting of the words
"Bantam Books" and the portrayal of a rooster, is Registered in U.S. Patent
and Trademark Office and in other countries. Marca Registrada. Bantam
Books, 1540 Broadway, New York, New York 10036.*

PRINTED IN THE UNITED STATES OF AMERICA

OPM   0 9 8 7 6 5 4 3 2 1

Dear Reader,

In the legend of Pandora, Pandora gave in to curiosity, peeked into a box she'd been warned never to open, and accidentally let loose all the evils that now plague mankind. For me, however, the real heart of the story has always been that Pandora managed to close the box again before "hope" escaped. Hope was thus saved and remains a comfort to men and women everywhere.

My Pandora, Linnea Bryan, is led by her ever-growing curiosity to expose several secrets to the light of day. In a more modern, rural turn of phrase, she "opens up a real can of worms" when she returns to her mother's hometown and begins to ask questions about her family's past. She's also curious about her handsome, enigmatic neighbor, Marsh Austin. As in Pandora's case, the results of Linnea's quest for knowledge aren't all pleasant, but Linnea does manage to remain an optimist. Since she, like Pandora, never stops hoping for the best, she is able to deal with a difficult situation and also have a positive effect on those around her, especially Marsh.

I hope you enjoy reading my modern Pandora's story as much as I enjoyed writing it.

Kathy Lynn Emerson

ONE

The house next door had been standing empty for nearly fifteen years. Boarded up, abandoned, forlorn looking, it had passed into the category of eyesore a long time ago. The obvious solution was to tear it down.

That had been Marshall Austin's intention. He'd had plans to purchase the property, salvage what he could, and then level the building. Owning that land would have given him all the additional space he needed to breed and train his sled dogs.

Scowling fiercely, he cursed his bad timing. Thanks to his recent interest in the property, Linnea Bryan had been reminded that she owned a house in rural Maine. Now she was coming to take a look at it. According to the lawyer Marsh had talked to, she thought she could get a better price than he was offering by having the place fixed up before she sold it.

Just like her mother, Marsh decided. Greedy. Out

for number one. No concern for those whose lives she was throwing into chaos.

"You're going to bore holes in the bay window if you keep staring through it that way," Aunt Jen said to him. "Why on earth are you glowering at the Dennison house?"

"Dennison's granddaughter refused to sell."

At his back, Marsh heard the faint whir of his aunt's wheelchair as it glided around the dining-room table. A moment later she edged in next to him, and he could smell the delicate floral scent she favored.

"Why?" Jen asked.

"I couldn't offer her enough money." Bitterness laced his words and he had to control the urge to fist his hands. There never seemed to be enough cash on hand. He was doing okay, but he wouldn't be for long if he overextended his resources.

Damn the woman! What perverse impulse was motivating her? She'd never shown any interest in her inheritance before.

"No one's likely to offer her a better deal." Aunt Jen's soothing voice cut through his dark mood like a shaft of sunlight on a cloudy day. "Just be patient and she'll change her mind."

Would she? he wondered. Not if she was anything like her mother, she wouldn't. Denise had been tenacious as a terrier, only one of the characteristics she shared with the species.

"She's coming here," he said aloud.

"Well, then," Jen said in a cheerful voice, "you

have nothing to worry about. She'll take one look, see what a wreck the place is, and accept your offer."

The view through the window supported Jen's opinion, but Marsh had a bad feeling about this. "She never once came to Austin's Crossing when her grandfather was alive. Why bother now?"

"I expect you can find out, dear."

Turning, Marsh forced a smile for his aunt's sake. He sat on the window seat so she wouldn't have to crane her neck to look up at him. Although Jen beamed back at him with her usual toothy grin, Marsh's smile faltered. She was too thin. And gray streaked her dark hair. Her face had the pinched look that came from enduring almost constant pain. For the moment, however, all her attention was fixed on finding a solution to the problem of Linnea Bryan.

"Wouldn't any of your former associates be able to uncover some details on her financial status?" Jen asked. "A few phone calls, one or two favors called in, and you could have a complete background report." She hesitated, then added, "They *owe* you."

Uncomfortable with that idea, Marsh hesitated. Debt didn't come into it. More crucial was his reluctance to trigger memories of the eleven years he'd spent in police work and what they had cost him. He no longer had full use of his left arm, and hip-replacement surgery had left him with a permanent limp.

"Bad idea?" Jen asked.

In the two years he'd been back in Austin's Crossing, the two of them had moved beyond the parameters of aunt and nephew and had become friends. The sixteen-year difference in their ages had been bridged. And with Jen's help he was building a good relationship with the third member of their household, his nine-year-old half sister, Cassie.

Jen had suffered far worse injuries than his, he reminded himself, and had been left with much greater dependence upon others too. Her unceasingly positive outlook on life had been an inspiration to him, easing the torment of his darkest moments. Her ability to remain optimistic in the face of all her difficulties continued to amaze him.

And her advice was sound. He still had a couple of very good friends in law enforcement. If he asked, they'd help.

"No, it's a good idea, Aunt Jen. Forewarned is forearmed. Give me a few hours and I'll know all kinds of things about Linnea Bryan, right down to and including the color of her underwear."

"Surely this investigation doesn't need to go into quite that much detail, dear. I didn't intend that you invade her privacy." Jen's tone was prim but her eyes were twinkling, reflecting her relief that he was able to joke about the kind of contacts he had.

Not so very long ago, any mention of his former career would put him in a dark, despondent mood for hours. Nowadays he didn't have time to brood. Not about his injuries and not about Linnea Bryan, either.

"You never know what information will turn out to be important," he said with mock solemnity.

Just for the hell of it, he'd have to see if he could

find out what color undies she favored. It was amazing the amount of personal information one could glean from credit-card records.

"Take a right at the refrigerator." Repeated aloud, the directions she'd been given sounded even more unlikely.

Linnea Bryan's expression was doubtful as she scanned the shoulder of the road. Then she saw it. Avocado green and doorless, the predicted household appliance appeared, incongruously rising out of a tuft of tall grass. It was tilted at a slight angle, as if to point the way.

Linnea slowed her red classic Mustang convertible to a stop, wondering if she really wanted to turn onto the narrow, winding dirt road. There were no signs to tell her where it led. She had only the word of a taciturn gas-station attendant ten miles back to assure her that she was going to end up in Austin's Crossing.

A map would have been an excellent idea. Not making this trip at all might have been even smarter, but she hadn't had a whole lot of choice. That morning, certain that finding her destination would be a simple matter, she'd blithely left both the Maine Turnpike and civilization behind and had headed into the wilds.

"You can't miss it," her grandfather's lawyer had assured her.

Hah! That three-piece suit had never bothered to visit the house in person. He'd given orders over the phone to have it boarded up, following her mother's instructions, since Linnea had been only thirteen when she'd inherited the place. She'd completely forgotten she owned it until recently.

As she turned onto the dirt road Linnea wondered why her grandfather had made the long trek to that plush office in Portland to put his affairs in order. Surely there were attorneys closer at hand. A frown creased her brow as she bumped slowly along, determined that this washboard road would not damage her car.

Both frowns and bumpy roads were becoming familiar to her, she thought with a hint of irony. Certainly her carefully laid out career plans had hit a major pothole. The job security she'd believed was hers had vanished overnight when her middle-management position had been wiped out by corporate downsizing.

Think about something positive, she told herself as she swerved around a downed tree limb in the middle of the road. Getting depressed about her situation wouldn't help anything.

She concentrated on her house.

That house was going to sell for a quick profit.

With the resulting nest egg, she'd have enough to pay her bills for a few months, until she could find another job. Linnea was encouraged by the fact that she'd already had one offer on the place. Ridiculously low, of course. But still, if one person was interested in buying, there would be others.

Considerably cheered, she kept driving.

Ten minutes later Linnea came upon a cluster of buildings. With no town-line marker to tip her off, she might have driven right through, a feat that could have been accomplished in little more than the blink of an eye, but she'd been warned. The entire community contained only nineteen houses, one church, an abandoned one-room schoolhouse built in the previous century, a post office, and what the lawyer had called a "mom-and-pop" store. This had to be Austin's Crossing.

A faded sign over the door of a minuscule post office confirmed her deduction. Linnea pulled into the small parking lot and was about to get out of the car when she noticed the boldly lettered sign on the door: CLOSED FOR LUNCH. BACK AT ONE.

A glance at her watch told her she'd have a twenty-minute wait if she wanted the postmaster to identify which house was hers. In a town this size, she suspected she could probably go door-to-door until she found someone at home to ask, but it seemed more efficient to take her question to the convenience store adjacent to the post office.

While she slipped her sunglasses into their case and finger-combed her short dark hair, Linnea eyed the rustic clapboard building. The sign over the door identified it as the Austin's Crossing Market.

A flash of red first caught Marsh's attention. He glanced up from the refrigerated case he was restocking to peer through the notice-littered plate-glass window at the front of the store.

Not just red. Flame red. The brilliant summer sunshine accentuated the eye-popping paint job.

After he slid the last two-liter bottle of soda onto the shelf, Marsh closed the glass door and retrieved the cardboard box he'd just emptied. Only then did he give his full attention to the driver, narrowing his eyes to study her as she got out of the car and headed his way.

He knew who she was, if only because she looked as out of place as her car did.

"City" was written all over her, from her pointy-toed shoes to the expensive little dress she was wearing. Its stylish length drew his attention to a great set of legs.

Frowning, Marsh told himself she wasn't worth a second look . . . but he looked anyway. Skinny, he decided. With no bosom to speak of. Not his type at all. And her straight, blue-black hair was cut so short, the wind had barely ruffled it while she'd driven there. He preferred long hair on a woman, something he could run his fingers through.

An unwelcome image invaded his thoughts—long dark hair hanging down a woman's back all the way to her hips.

Denise's hair.

Denise Dennison, Linnea Bryan's mother, had been Marsh's baby-sitter from the time he was a few months old until her abrupt departure from Austin's Crossing when he was five. He'd thought she was wonderful, especially when she hugged him and let him bury his face in those thick, sweetly scented locks.

Unfortunately, Marsh's father had felt the same way about her.

Shaking off the memory, Marsh eyed Denise's daughter with a considering gaze. His friends on the force had come through. He had the basics. Linnea Bryan had time on her hands because she'd just lost her job. It hadn't sounded as if she had any serious money problems, though. After all, she could always go work for her mother.

A bit of deeper digging had turned up the surprising fact that Denise had made a success of herself after leaving Maine. These days she owned and operated a small software company in California.

Light footsteps tapped across the wooden floor of the little porch in front of Marsh's window. As Linnea passed by, no doubt unaware of him watching her from the other side of the glass, he caught an intriguing close-up glimpse of a turned-up nose, long eyelashes, and aquamarine eyes.

The same color she favored in her underwear.

"Well, hell," he muttered.

Refusing to be caught gaping at her like an infatuated schoolboy, Marsh abruptly headed for the back of the store. He had work to do, he told himself. And Denise Dennison's daughter was the last person he intended to allow to distract him.

❖―――❖

A bell tinkled as Linnea entered the store. The old-fashioned sound and a decor to match brought a delighted smile to her lips. Just inside the door and to her right was a wooden counter with a high, padded stool behind it. All it lacked was a gnarled old codger sitting there to guard the cash register, the racks of cigarettes, and the microwave.

Attached to the microwave was a sign offering to heat up Hot Pockets and English-muffin pizzas. Linnea realized she was hungry, in spite of the large, late breakfast she'd indulged in en route. The faint, lingering aroma of freshly perked coffee made her long for a cup of that, too, but she saw no sign of a pot.

As curious as she was peckish, Linnea surveyed her surroundings. The store was small but jam-packed. There didn't seem to be much that wasn't stocked. Just to the left of the entrance, next to the candy display, was a newspaper rack featuring a selection of dailies from around the state. Bangor, Waterville, Lewiston, Augusta, and Portland were all represented . . . each by one copy.

A thunking sound alerted her to the location of the proprietor. She chose an aisle that balanced pet food, canned vegetables, and tins of corned beef and tuna fish on one side, with paper products and pasta on the other, and followed it toward the rear of the store.

A man in jeans and a dark blue T-shirt had his back to her. With fluid movements sufficient to stop Linnea in her tracks, he reached up, took hold of a large carton of paper towels stored on a shelf just above his head, and lifted it down.

He was one of the most outstanding male speci-
mens Linnea had ever seen. Muscular without being
musclebound, he radiated strength. Her admiring
gaze slid over a tight butt and long, solid legs as he
bent at the waist to place the carton on the floor.
When he stood upright again, she took note of hair
that was dark brown and wavy. He wore it long, tied in
a queue at the nape of his neck.

Flexing fingers drew her attention, briefly, to his
left hand. He stretched his arm, limbering it up as if
he'd pulled a muscle while hefting the box.

Without looking around to see who had come into
his store, he spoke. "Something I can do for you?"

Oh, yes, she wanted to say.

His voice was even better than she'd expected, and
a good match for all that fine packaging. Deep and
mellow, it made her think of molasses pouring slowly
out of a jar.

Linnea held her breath when he started to turn
around. So far he'd been too perfect. There had to be
a flaw somewhere. But his features, while not exactly
handsome, were intriguing. His lips had a decidedly
sensual appeal and his eyes were the color of maple
syrup. She looked deeply into them, searching for
some sign that he, too, was feeling this immediate and
undeniable sexual attraction.

Instead she found implacable mistrust. A wave of
suspicion flowed toward her, strong enough to make
her back up a step and draw in a startled breath.

Reality rushed to the fore, and with it her common
sense. What an absurd reaction to have to a complete

stranger. Out of character for her too. For one un-
guarded moment whatever sophistication she'd acquired over the years had been jerked out from under
her. She'd obviously lost her perspective, as well as
any instinct for self-preservation, right along with her
career.

Despite his steady, unnerving gaze, Linnea tried
for a firmer grip on her self-control. The last thing she
needed was to be attracted to a man. Any man. Least
of all one who lived in this godforsaken little town.
This was neither the time nor the place for a fling.

Especially not the place.

"Something I can do for you?" he asked again.

With an effort, Linnea pulled herself together and
managed to answer his question. "I'm looking for the
Dennison house. Can you tell me which one it is?"

No surprise showed in his expression. No curiosity, either. It was as if he already knew who she was
and why she'd come to Austin's Crossing.

Acutely aware that he radiated a dangerous intensity, she also got the distinct impression that he was
barely in command of a tightly leashed anger. She
couldn't begin to guess at its cause, but she did know
that he was not a man she'd want to meet in a dark
alley.

Not unless he was on *her* side.

Apparently deciding she'd been sufficiently cowed,
he answered her question. His manner was brusque, as
if he couldn't wait to get rid of her.

"Turn right as you leave the parking lot. Your
house is the third one on the left."

"Thank you." Intimidated but determined not to let him see her squirm, Linnea managed a regal nod and took a moment to glance at the offerings at the back of the store. Off to her right was a combination deli, bakery, and meat counter. Her mouth watered at the sight of cherry cheesecake and other delights under glass.

"You've wasted your time coming here."

She blinked, startled by his blunt words and jolted by his threatening tone of voice. All thoughts of food vanished.

"The Dennison place is too far gone to save," he went on. "It's been neglected for more than a decade. Your best course, city girl, is to take the offer you've already had and go back where you came from."

Girl?

Who did he think he was?

Reacting to the insult implicit in his warning, Linnea went on the defensive. Drawing herself up a little straighter, she sent him a cold look. Her words were clipped and even icier than her glare. "I don't believe what I do with my property is any of your business."

She intended to follow this sharp put-down by stalking off, but he stepped into the aisle to block her escape route. She nearly ran into him, and even though she averted a collision, she ended up standing so close to him that she had to look up to meet his eyes.

They'd be at eye level if she'd worn heels, she thought.

That knowledge was insufficient to counter the

daunting impact his nearness had on her senses. Strangely, she was not afraid of him, just very aware of the apparent strength of his arms, the width of his shoulders, the faint, clean scent of Ivory soap and spicy aftershave.

Once again, she was forced to acknowledge her purely physical response to the splendid male animal before her. She had to take a firm grip on her wayward thoughts. As they stared at each other, neither flinching, for a long, tense moment, she ordered herself to pretend indifference.

She managed to hold her ground, refusing to let him see just how much he unnerved her. She schooled her facial muscles into a haughty expression, but even as she did so she wondered at her own reactions. She wasn't behaving at all in her normal manner. Linnea Bryan was renowned in the business community of Albany, New York, for her ability to take a rational approach with even the most aggravating adversary.

So why was she suddenly uncertain what words were going to pop out of her own mouth next? Rather than risk saying the wrong thing, she kept silent, waiting for him to respond to what she'd already said.

"Everything in this town is my business." The simmering anger had been replaced by a stolid implacability that infused his voice with authority. John Wayne confronting the bad guys. Darth Vader ordering the fate of the galaxy. "We look out for each other in Austin's Crossing," he added.

"How comforting."

Linnea recognized her terse, sarcastic rejoinder for

what it was—a feeble attempt to hide an even less acceptable response to his words. For a fleeting moment she'd imagined just how it would feel to have a man like this one "look out" for her.

"I'm Marshall Austin."

"Am I supposed to be impressed that you and the town share the same name?"

A laconic note came into his voice. "Couldn't hurt."

"Well I'm not. And that minor detail hardly gives you the right to behave like some kind of feudal overlord."

His quick, slashing grin rocked her, for it left her with the clear impression that he knew exactly what rights medieval noblemen had once held over their female serfs.

The expression that replaced it a moment later was equally unsettling, a grimly determined look that boded ill for anyone who dared stand in Marshall Austin's way.

"Take my advice, Miss Bryan. Don't stick around any longer than necessary. This town has nothing to offer you."

"You know my name." Somehow that was more disconcerting than anything that had gone before.

"Yes, I do. In fact, I know quite a lot about you."

Linnea took a moment to collect her thoughts. She had the uneasy feeling she had just been given until sundown to get out of Dodge. "Is Marshall your name . . . or your title? I wouldn't think a burg this small would rate any higher officer than a part-time constable."

One corner of his mobile mouth twitched at her acerbic response, as if he had to acknowledge the accuracy of her gibe. Linnea realized she was holding her breath and let it out.

"See for yourself the condition your grandfather's house is in," he said, his expression now completely enigmatic.

"Thank you," she replied. "I intend to."

How absurd! she thought as he stepped aside to let her pass. She was feeling disappointed because he'd brought their verbal sparring match to an end. She'd expected him to respond to her play on words by telling her this town wasn't big enough for both of them. Instead he'd apparently grown bored with her. She'd been dismissed.

She was about to stalk out of the store when the missing piece in the puzzle of all this hostility suddenly snapped into place. Whirling around, she faced him once again, and this time she was the one to shoot daggers in his direction. Her voice reflected both her exasperation and her outrage.

"You're the one who made that insultingly low offer!"

"No secret there." The laconic drawl was back, but his eyes held a new wariness.

Irritating man!

"Then I suppose I should apologize for not recognizing your name." Her words all but dripped sarcasm, and she barely contained the urge to sniff disdainfully. "The amount was so small that I didn't pay any attention to such minor details."

"Take my word for it," Marshall Austin said. "That's the best deal you're going to get."

"I wouldn't take your word for it that the sun is shining," she informed him, "and I wouldn't sell my grandfather's house to you now if you were the last prospective buyer on the face of the earth!"

TWO

"Well, hell," Marsh muttered.

With a fine air of melodrama, Linnea Bryan had just stormed out of his store.

That wasn't the way things were supposed to go.

Disgusted with himself, Marsh limped along in her wake, stopping at the front counter to extract the telephone from the shelf beneath. The engine of her sporty little car roared to life as he punched in the number for home. The ringing sound was underscored by that of gravel spattering out from under her tires as she sped out of the parking lot.

The lady had a temper.

"She's on her way," Marsh announced as soon as his aunt said hello.

"What's she like?"

"Reminds me of her mother."

Why had he said that? Marsh's free hand curled into a fist. He hadn't wanted anyone, not even Aunt

Jen, to start speculating about the events of all those years ago.

"I remember Denise slightly," his aunt said thoughtfully. "She was four or five years younger than I was."

Which meant Jen would have been away at college at the time of his parents' divorce. It was possible she had never been told there was any connection between seventeen-year-old Denise Dennison's abrupt departure from Austin's Crossing and the breakup of the Austins' marriage. Marsh held back a sigh of relief. He hadn't been sure how much Jen knew. He'd been too young himself at the time to understand more than his mother's tears and his father's anger. Neither one of them had been inclined to talk about the split afterward, but Marsh had picked up clues, enough guidance to conclude that Denise was to blame for what had happened.

She'd been the first woman to deceive him, the first person in his life to reject him in favor of bright city lights.

"Marsh?"

His aunt's voice jerked him back to the matter at hand.

"Did you hear me? Exactly how is Linnea like her mother?"

I'm drawn to her. Not the way a five-year-old was to his teenage baby-sitter, though. This was definitely adult male to full-grown woman.

Aloud, he said only, "She's . . . feisty."

A momentary silence greeted that announcement.

"You do know that the word *feisty* is not a compliment?" Aunt Jen was into crossword puzzles, when she had time in her busy daily routine. "A feist originally meant any small, bad-tempered dog."

"That fits." Cynicism made his voice harsh.

Or maybe it was irritation . . . at himself. He'd been rude to Linnea. Worse, he'd actually tried to scare her off. All because some indefinable quality about her *attracted* him.

"Oh, dear," his aunt murmured. "you two clashed, didn't you? Did you try to browbeat the girl? That's no way to get her to sell to you."

"I'm open to suggestions, Aunt Jen."

"Well, dear, you could try sweet-talking her."

Denise's daughter? "I'd sooner let a viper into my bed."

"No one's asking you to seduce her, dear." Her voice tinged with asperity, Aunt Jen clarified: "I simply meant that you're a very good-looking man, and that you can be charming when you put your mind to it."

A graphic scene began to play in his mind's eye, filled with snake charmers and belly dancers. He quickly banished it. He was not a man given to daydreaming, especially not some fantastic version of the Arabian nights. It annoyed him even more to realize that this brief foray into fantasy had gotten him hot.

One more reason to damn Linnea Bryan. He'd never had any trouble controlling his libido before she came along.

That's what came of no social life. Not only did he

pant after the first thing in skirts, but he'd obviously
lost his carefully honed policeman's ability to size people up. There'd been a time when he could do that,
quickly and accurately, with anyone he met. No more.
After their brief encounter, he honestly didn't know
what to make of Linnea Bryan. Or his own uncharac-
teristically hostile behavior toward her.

It was true he wanted her land, but getting it
wasn't a matter of life and death. Hell, it wasn't even
necessary for his economic survival. Although he
wasn't ready to throw in the towel quite yet, he acknowledged that it would be just as good for the community to have the Dennison place fixed up and sold
to some nice family.

"If you're thinking the limp detracts, you're a
fool."

"What?" He'd been so lost in his thoughts, he
hadn't heard what Jen said.

"Some women find wounded heroes romantic,"
she added, and he realized she'd misinterpreted his
long silence.

"You're getting ahead of yourself, Aunt Jen. I'm
betting she takes one good look at the house and high-
tails it right back to where she came from."

He dismissed the idea of romancing Linnea's
property out of her just as he'd already dismissed her
parting shot. Women like Denise Dennison said a lot
of things they didn't mean, and Linnea was her
mother's daughter. There was a good chance she'd
change her mind about selling to him.

"I wonder—" Jen broke off as, through the phone line, she heard the sound of the bell over the store's door.

"Got to go, Aunt Jen," Marsh told her, though it was only the postmaster who'd come in. It was his habit to buy a candy bar for dessert on his way back to work after lunch. He didn't need Marsh's assistance, but it was a convenient excuse for Marsh to end the conversation before he had to listen to any more of Jen's helpful suggestions.

He'd handled Linnea Bryan badly. He knew that. No finesse at all. And now that he was thinking with his mind instead of other parts of his body, he knew exactly why he'd overreacted.

He'd been caught off guard, made defensive and angry and blunt, by the unacceptable, unpalatable, irrational, inescapable fact that he was physically attracted to Denise Dennison's daughter.

Just as his father had been attracted to Denise.

Marsh wondered if there was some genetic failing in Austin men that accounted for the phenomenon.

It didn't matter. He was stronger than his father had been. Besides, as he'd told Aunt Jen, he'd lay odds Linnea would be long gone by the time he got home from work. Tomorrow, he'd call her lawyer and make another offer. Hell, he'd be generous and make it a couple of hundred dollars higher. That should help take the curse off her having to eat her own words.

And if she didn't accept his offer, then that would be the end of it.

Romance Linnea Bryan to get her to sell him her house?

No way. He had too many scars already.

Hot, tired, discouraged, and *hungry*, Linnea sank down on the third step of the stairs inside her house, rested her chin on the heels of both hands, and glared at a strip of curled and peeling wallpaper stained with mildew. Paper hung from the ceiling too. Rodent droppings adorned the dust-covered floor in the entryway.

A long, shuddering sigh escaped her control and echoed in the stairwell.

Marshall Austin had been right about the place, as she'd suspected he might be from the moment she pulled up in front of her grandfather's house and took her first good, hard look at it. Dilapidated and forlorn in the bright summer sun, all its windows boarded up, it was a dismal sight made even less appealing by a sagging porch and the undeniable fact that the whole structure was badly in need of paint.

So much for making a quick sale and getting enough money to live on until she found another job.

"What a dump," she quoted under her breath.

As if in answer, her stomach growled loudly, as it had been doing periodically during her room-by-room tour of her inheritance. She wished she hadn't already eaten her emergency candy bar. Even more, she wished she'd had the foresight to buy a few provisions at the Austin's Crossing Market . . . before she clashed with its owner.

It might also have been wise to humor Marshall Austin concerning the sale of this house. Even though his offer was way too low to be considered, given her present financial straits, keeping his goodwill in what was obviously a small, tight-knit community would have been the smart thing to do.

Too late now.

That ship had sailed.

Her best bet was to get out of there and find a phone and food, not necessarily in that order. She was glad she'd at least had the foresight to bring her small overnight bag inside the house with her. Before beginning her explorations, she'd changed into jeans and a loose, sleeveless cotton blouse, shedding the dress she'd put on for her early-morning appointment with her grandfather's lawyer. She'd kept the same shoes, which now drew patterns in the dust on the stair riser. The flats were stylish, expensive, and imported, but they were also the most comfortable footwear Linnea had ever owned.

She believed in being comfortable, which was part of what made her present predicament so galling. She'd left behind a cozy cocoon, her condo in Albany. Childlike, she wanted her security blanket back.

Spoiled child, she corrected herself. Linnea was good at searing self-analysis. Too good, sometimes, for her own peace of mind. Fighting the weak and cowardly urge to stay right where she was and feel sorry for herself, maybe even indulge in a good cry over the unjustness of fate, she abruptly stood.

Dust motes danced in a beam of sunlight at her sudden movement, and her unexpected pleasure at the sight was bracing. What was called for here, she told herself sternly, was an attitude adjustment. She needed to change her way of thinking. Negativity accomplished nothing.

The entire place had been beautiful once. Fixed up, she was sure it could be again. That meant, with hard work and a bit of ingenuity, she could still sell it at a decent price.

Even her untrained eye could see it was going to be a major undertaking. She knew there was only one course to follow if she was to succeed. In order to afford the extensive repairs the house required, she'd have to live in it during the renovation. And even then she'd have to do most of the work herself to cut down on costs.

Preposterous as the idea seemed at first, Linnea was all but committed to it by the time she completed her second walk-through and returned to the first floor. Something about the place appealed to her, despite its present state of neglect and disrepair. And she didn't really have any other choice.

Mentally making a list of pros and cons, Linnea decided the biggest plus was that the roof didn't leak. She'd found the attic dry as a bone, even if it was hot enough up there to leave her gasping for breath.

The biggest minus was Marshall Austin.

Also hot enough to leave her gasping for breath.

Forget him.

As far as she knew, no one else in this small town had any reason to be unfriendly toward her. Certain she'd be able to fit in perfectly well, even though she'd never lived in a rural area before, Linnea started to make specific plans. She was adaptable.

Lord knew, with her mother, she'd had to be.

A sense of purpose buoyed her spirits as she stuffed her discarded dress and hose into the small suitcase. She knew a young couple who would be delighted to sublet her condo, furnished, even for so brief a period as a few months. They'd move in tomorrow if she'd let them. They'd been hoping for a vacancy in her building for months in order to be near the husband's sister and brother-in-law.

That would give her the cash she'd need to purchase wallpaper and other redecorating materials. First, though, she had to have a phone installed and the power turned on.

At her car, the overnight bag stowed once more, she turned to look back at her new home. The neglect was even more vividly apparent when she compared her place with its nearest neighbor.

The exteriors of the two houses were subtly different, no doubt due to alterations that had been made over the years, but certain similarities remained. Unmistakably, the well-cared-for house next door was her property's better-looking twin.

Linnea was so busy staring at the building that she didn't notice the two figures walking toward her along the sidewalk until they were only a few feet away. One was a girl who appeared to be about nine or ten years old. The other was a large, black dog. Linnea froze when she spotted the animal, then forced herself to relax.

The girl was on the thin side, neatly dressed in cutoff jeans and a T-shirt that proclaimed her a fan of the Portland Sea Dogs. Her long light brown hair was baby-fine and had nearly slipped free of the coated elastic band holding it back in a ponytail.

When she was a foot from Linnea, she halted, one hand idly stroking the dog's compact and well-furred body. In the other hand she held an apple. She took a bite, chewed, and swallowed before she spoke.

"Hi."

"Hi, yourself." Linnea's focus remained on the dog, her nervousness about what it might do strong enough to distract her from both the girl and the sight of food. She forced her lips into the semblance of a smile, telling herself that the animal was obviously a pet. The child had it under control. There was no reason to be upset.

"I'm Cassie Graham."

The dog's tongue lolled out in what Linnea hoped was a friendly greeting, but she continued to keep a wary distance as she introduced herself. She'd been bitten by dogs twice, and she had no desire to repeat the experience. Her contact with children, friendly or otherwise, was less traumatic but just as limited.

"You can pet him if you want," Cassie invited.

Tentatively, Linnea extended one hand and touched the soft, silky fur. When the dog made no threatening moves or sounds, she steeled herself to scratch behind his ear. Although she couldn't think why it should matter to her, she didn't want Cassie to think she was a coward.

Apparently, her attention pleased the dog. His lolling tongue unwound even farther and he began to drool. Combined with peculiar eyes, one brown and one blue, were a pair of erect ears and a plume of a tail. The effect was comical and Cassie responded with a delighted giggle.

"He likes you, Linnea."

Reassured by the feeling that this particular pooch probably liked everybody, Linnea relaxed. Her smile was no longer forced. "What's his name?"

"Foolish."

"I beg your pardon?"

"My brother said he'd never seen a dog with a more foolish-looking expression on his face, so he named him Foolish."

It did fit. "What kind of dog is he?"

"He's a Siberian husky, of course."

"Of course." Linnea had the feeling she was missing some significant point, but at the moment it hardly seemed important. She gave Foolish a final pat and withdrew her hand.

"Are you going to move in next door?" Cassie asked.

"Looks that way," Linnea said. "Do you suppose I could use your phone?"

"I'll have to ask Aunt Jen."

Before Linnea could say another word, the child

bolted, racing toward the house. The dog stayed where he was, watching her hopefully. When she moved, Foolish moved with her.

"Nice puppy," Linnea murmured.

She wasn't prepared for the change in expression when he bared very sharp-looking teeth. She couldn't tell if it was supposed to be a doggy version of a grin, or something more threatening, and decided the better part of valor was to stay put until Cassie came back.

She used the time to make further comparisons between the two houses. Cassie's had a garage as well as a sturdy barn. Linnea's barn, which she had yet to explore, looked as if it would collapse in the next good wind.

Whistling for the dog, Cassie reappeared at the side entrance to her house. She motioned Linnea toward her. "Come on in. Aunt Jen says it's okay."

As at Linnea's house, the side door led into a small utility room connected to the outbuildings on one side and the kitchen on the other. To Linnea's relief, Cassie sent Foolish straight through into a fenced backyard, then escorted her new neighbor into the interior of the twin house.

The differences from that point on were legion. This was a home, lived in, loved, cared for. And at the center of the warmth was a small woman with a bright smile.

"This is Aunt Jen," Cassie said. "Aunt Jen, this is Linnea."

"Welcome, dear. Call me Jen and pardon me if I don't get up."

Taken aback by the bluntness, Linnea wasn't sure how to respond until she caught sight of the twinkle in Jen's eyes. "That looks like an outstanding example of state-of-the-art transportation you've got there."

"Best money could buy," Jen agreed, patting one wheel affectionately. "Indoor-outdoor electric scooter. And, so you don't have to be embarrassed about asking, I injured my spine in an accident about five years back. Can't use my legs, but the rest of me is doing just fine, thank you kindly."

That practical, no-nonsense attitude quickly put Linnea at ease. Ten minutes later, her phone calls out of the way, she was comfortably ensconced on the window seat in the dining room, studying the kitchen side of her own house while she tried not to wolf down the cookies Jen had set out to go with the tall, cold glass of lemonade she'd pressed upon her unexpected guest. Cassie was curled up in a chair in one corner with a book open on her lap, reading and listening at the same time.

"It's going to need a lot of work," the older woman pointed out.

"I plan to do most of it myself." Linnea hoped she sounded more confident than she felt. She was determined not to be discouraged this early on.

"If you don't mind my saying so, dear, you don't look like the sort of person who's had much experience scraping old paint off clapboards."

Scraping? Linnea glanced at her house again, at the peeling paint and the places where the boards themselves had come loose. This project might be a bit more involved than she'd thought. Still, what other option was there? She'd simply have to learn as she went along.

"Do you suppose the local library has any books on home repair?"

"I'm sure they must. Cassie can introduce you to the librarian. They're very good friends."

Then Jen's brow furrowed, and Linnea wondered if Jen intended to mount a serious campaign to talk her out of her plans. As she watched, the other woman seemed to come to a decision, and her expression smoothed out again. "So, tell us, dear. Exactly what do you have in mind?"

Briefly, Linnea sketched out her ideas. Sharing them with Jen and Cassie made them seem more real. Even though Jen still occasionally looked skeptical and was quick to point out several more areas where Linnea would have to hire expert help, Linnea began to take heart. She realized she was looking forward to the challenge of turning her battered old house into a showplace.

"First thing in the morning," she said, "I'll have to start contacting contractors to upgrade the wiring and plumbing."

"You'll want to have professionals inspect the chimney and the boiler too," Jen advised. "And there's no way you can stay in that house tonight."

For a moment Linnea thought Jen was about to invite her to stay with her and Cassie. Instead she recommended a motel in New Portsmouth.

"Is that the next town over?"

"That's the town. This is the village."

Linnea knew she looked blank.

"The town of New Portsmouth," Jen went on, "is a municipality, consisting of four villages. Austin's Crossing is one of them." By the time Jen finished explaining, she'd also produced a road map to show Linnea how to get where she was going by the most direct route.

"You should take a look around this place before you leave," Jen suggested. "Both houses were built at the same time, back before the Civil War. By two brothers, I believe. You'll have noticed already that they're similar."

"Yes. They must have been nearly identical once. I'd love to see what you've done with this one."

"Good. Cassie can give you the guided tour. My nephew rigged an apparatus on the stairs that lets me get back and forth between floors, but rather than go along, I believe I'll take a look in that bureau"—she indicated a heavy oak sideboard—"for some old photographs I remember seeing back a while. There should be at least one clear shot of your house in its heyday."

During the next ten minutes Linnea's determination to restore her house to its former glory grew. The excitement she felt surprised her, but she let it build. It had been a long time since she'd been this enthusiastic about anything, or had felt this alive.

She'd made the right decision. She was sure of it.

"This is my room," Cassie announced, throwing open a door on the second floor. One entire wall was filled with shelves. In addition to dolls and books, they contained several distinctive boxes.

"I see you like jigsaw puzzles, Cassie."

The girl nodded, but a bleak expression settled over her delicate features. "My brother used to work on them with me, but he's been too busy lately. It isn't as much fun to do one alone."

"I have a 3-D jigsaw puzzle I've been putting off starting," Linnea surprised herself by confiding. "Maybe you can help me with it after I get moved in."

Cassie brightened. "Cool," she said.

Linnea grinned. The more time she spent with the girl, the more comfortable she felt. In fact, Cassie was beginning to remind Linnea of herself as a child.

Poor thing.

Did Cassie have any friends her own age? Linnea wondered. The brother, obviously, was older. From what Linnea had observed, Cassie was isolated here, with only an adult and the dog for company. Linnea's situation growing up had been far different on the surface. After all, she'd always lived in densely popu-lated cities. But the result was the same. Like Cassie, she'd spent a lot of time in a quiet corner, reading. She'd developed an active imagination and had learned to entertain herself.

To cap off the tour, Linnea's young guide led her back through the kitchen and utility room and out into the yard on the other side of the house from

Linnea's place. Cassie had released Foolish into this area earlier, and Linnea glanced around nervously, looking for some sign of him.

"Time to meet the rest of the family," Cassie announced.

"Your brother?" Linnea guessed.

Based on Cassie's comments, she was expecting a teenager, a young man several years older than his sister. She'd accounted for Cassie's complaint that he was too busy to spend much time with her by reasoning that, since school was out for the summer, he probably had a part-time job.

Giggling, Cassie caught Linnea's hand and pulled her toward the nearest of what appeared to be several small storage sheds. "You can meet my brother later. Right now Foolish wants you to meet one of his."

As if in response to hearing his name, Foolish and a second dog raced around the end of one of the little buildings and bounded toward Linnea and Cassie. The animal with Foolish was just as big. Linnea hoped he was also just as friendly.

No sooner had she formed that thought than another movement caught her eye. The two animals weren't alone. More dogs were following them. Dozens of them.

"Oh, my God," she whispered as she came to an abrupt standstill. Those little sheds were kennels.

The dogs streaming toward her looked like nothing so much as a pack of wolves.

Linnea tried in vain to ward off a wave of stark terror. A part of her mind knew hers was an irrational fear. She could see these animals were harmless. Cassie was already wading into their midst, patting heads and scratching ears, accepting the exuberant canine affection being lavished upon her.

But there were so many of them. In spite of her resolve to remain calm, Linnea began to shake uncontrollably. Then the first of the pack reached her, about to pounce, and she lost all perspective. She didn't care if the beast meant to nuzzle her hand or bite it. She wasn't giving it a chance to do either. In a blind panic she turned and fled.

She managed only a half-dozen steps before she came up hard against a solid obstacle. Strong arms wrapped around her in an attempt to keep her upright, pulling her close to a decidedly masculine body. Eyes closed, she buried her face against a broad shoulder and clung.

For a moment, held tight and enveloped by a vaguely familiar scent, she felt safe, but then one of the dogs hit her from behind, its weight driving her even deeper into the man's embrace and sending them tumbling to the ground in a tangle of arms and legs.

She could feel the man's chest move as he shouted to the dogs. "Tatupu! Zappa! Down."

That commanding tone ensured instant obedience. The dogs backed off. Linnea carefully released her death grip on her rescuer's waist.

Then she swallowed hard, steeling herself to look at his face.

She'd recognized his voice, just as she'd belatedly

identified that uniquely appealing blend of soap and aftershave.

The man who had twisted to take the brunt of their fall, who even now was still cradling her against his sprawled body, was Marshall Austin.

THREE

Marsh took his time releasing her, yielding to the urge to savor the feel of a soft, warm woman held tight in his arms. Once the dogs backed off, he had to let her go, and she squirmed until she managed to sit up, but until then he let himself imagine he had a right to cuddle and caress her.

His own thoughts shocked him into jerking his hand away from her bare arm. She'd changed out of the city clothes into jeans that hugged her slim hips like a second skin.

"You." She whispered the word as an accusation, but her flushed face and wide eyes gave her away. She was as aware of him as he was of her.

"Me." He waited, curious to find out what she'd do next.

When Emma, the woman who lived in the apartment above the store and worked for him part-time, had relieved him for the day, he'd come straight

home, anxious to discover how Linnea Bryan had re-
acted to her house. Now he was even more intrigued
by her reaction to him. Once she'd finished untan-
gling herself, she scooted away on her backside.

With an economy of motion, Marsh heaved himself upright and offered her his hand to help her rise.
Apparently at a loss for words, she glared at him and
batted his hand away.

"Suit yourself," he said.

Struggling to her feet, she seemed prepared to
square off against him . . . until she remembered the
dogs. The animals had removed themselves only a
short distance at his command. At the sight of them,
she hesitated, then glared at Marsh.

"You probably have them trained to attack," she
muttered.

"Scared?"

"I have reason to be."

It annoyed Marsh to find that the credo ingrained
in him during ten years of police work, the code that
obliged him to protect and serve the public, even
when that public didn't deserve his help, still had a
strong influence over him. Denise's daughter didn't
deserve any consideration from him, yet even with her
he wasn't able to banish his protective instincts completely.

"They won't attack you, and they don't bite." He
knew what it was to be afraid. "No need to be skittish
around them."

Before Linnea could make any response, Cassie
rushed up to them. "Aren't the dogs great, Linnea?"

"They're . . . something." Her carefully neutral tone surprised him. He hadn't expected her to be sensitive to Cassie's feelings.

"This is my big brother, Marsh." Cassie hurried into the introduction, oblivious of the tension between the two adults. "Marsh, this is Linnea."

"We've met, short stuff." He tugged affectionately on his sister's ponytail, all the while keeping his eyes on Linnea. "You look surprised, Miss Bryan. I take it you didn't know I was your grandfather's next-door neighbor?"

"What surprises me is that you're Cassie's brother."

Although she might mean only that he was a lot older than Cassie, or that the two of them had different last names, Marsh sensed Linnea's confusion came from the contrast between Cassie's puppy-dog friendliness and his tendency to snap at her.

"Linnea is moving into the old Dennison place," Cassie announced.

"Having it fixed up, you mean." Marsh was careful to keep his voice level and his expression bland. There was no excuse for them sniping at each other in front of a child.

Linnea drew herself up a bit straighter and frowned at him anyway, as if she knew he didn't put much stock in her vow to sell to anyone but him. "Your sister has been kind enough to show me around your house, to give me ideas for my own renovations. She's a very good tour guide."

"You didn't get to see the kennels," Cassie cut in.

"I don't believe Miss Bryan cares for dogs," Marsh murmured.

Ignoring him, Linnea spoke to Cassie. "I'm not accustomed to being around animals," she explained. "How many of them are there, anyway?"

"Thirty-five."

Only because he was watching her face so carefully did Marsh see her blanch. She betrayed no other overt distress. If she was as unnerved by dogs as he suspected, he had to admire her fortitude. By making light of her fear to Cassie, she'd knowingly exposed herself to further overtures from Cassie's canine friends.

"They're all Siberian huskies," Cassie continued. "Sled dogs. Marsh races them. And takes people on dogsled trips."

"How . . . interesting." Linnea seemed at a loss for words, but after a moment she managed a smile and went on in a hearty tone. "I guess I'll have to get used to hearing barking."

"Oh, they hardly ever bark," Cassie said. "They're trained not to. And they have very sweet temperaments. You'll love them once you get used to them."

"Don't count on Miss Bryan being here all that long," Marsh said.

"Four months."

"What?" He turned to Linnea.

"Four months," she said. "That's how long I'm staying. But now, as much as I've enjoyed this visit, I need to be on my way. See you tomorrow, Cassie."

With a quick hug of farewell to her new friend,

Cassie bounded off with a dozen of the dogs following at her heels.

Thunderstruck, Marsh struggled to take in what he was hearing. He'd accepted that he'd lost the land. He'd even started to look forward to seeing the Dennison place spruced up, to having new neighbors. Maybe some kids for Cassie to hang out with. But *Linnea* living right next door? For four months?

"Why?" he demanded. "Why are you staying?"

"I'll be doing most of the renovation work myself."

"Lady, you have got to be out of your mind."

"Neither my mental state nor what I do on my own property is any of your concern. Back off . . . Marshall."

At her tone, his eyes narrowed. "Give it up," he warned. "You can't possibly fix everything that's wrong with the Dennison house in four months."

"Don't be so sure of that," she shot back. "If I don't succeed in that length of time, it won't be for lack of trying."

"You are a trying woman, no doubt about that."

Hands on her hips, eyes flashing angry fire, she seemed about to give him further proof of it when Aunt Jen interrupted, calling to them from the open shed door. She was waving something square.

"Oh, she's found the photograph." Forgetting all about him, Linnea sent a bright smile toward Jen and started back across the lawn.

"Wait a minute."

She spared him a glance over her shoulder, probably to utter another put-down, but all at once her expression changed. She turned to face him fully, giving him time to catch up with her. Her expressive eyes betrayed genuine concern.

"You hurt your leg when I knocked you down. Why didn't you say something? I'm so sorry. I never stopped to think—"

"You didn't do a thing to me."

"Well, I know it was really the dogs, but if I hadn't tried to run away from them—"

"I said it wasn't your fault!"

"But you're limping."

"Yes, Miss Bryan, I am limping. I have limped for a good long time now and will for the rest of my life. Whatever else you may have done, you are not responsible for the injury to my leg."

Clearly upset by his harsh, brittle words, she started to speak, then pressed her lips together. Though he didn't want to see it there, he recognized empathy for his pain lurking in the depths of her aquamarine eyes. He regretted the loss when it vanished, wiped out by the return of her annoyance. After a last fulminating glare at him, she shifted her attention to Jen.

"Is that the picture?" she asked, continuing on to the open door.

Bright-eyed, Jen sent a curious look in his direction before answering Linnea. "Yes, it is." She handed it over. "What do you think?"

Marsh came up on the other side of his aunt as the two women studied the cardboard-backed photograph

Linnea held. The sepia print showed both houses, and judging by the clothing on the people who posed on their porches, it had been taken at the turn of the century.

"There don't seem to be any other houses nearby," Linnea said.

"No," Jen agreed. "I remember hearing that for a long while there were only two or three in all of Austin's Crossing. Austins, naturally. Other families came later."

"Why do you suppose they built them so close together?" Linnea wondered aloud. "You'd think if they had the space they'd want a little more privacy."

"It's a common enough phenomenon," Jen said. "At least in these parts. Two identical houses were often built side by side or on opposite sides of the road from each other. Sometimes two brothers built them. Sometimes it was a son or daughter who got married but didn't want to be too far away from the parents. Families liked to stick together in the old days. Sometimes economic necessity encouraged them to."

"Always an incentive," Marsh muttered under his breath.

Linnea ignored him.

After a long, piercing look at both of them, Jen chuckled. "Then, too, those were the days when everyone went to church on Sunday and it is one of the Ten Commandments to love thy neighbor."

"How times have changed," Linnea murmured.

And not for the better, Marsh thought as he abruptly turned away. His leg was throbbing, and he swore he could feel her eyes tracking his every painful step.

Love thy neighbor?

His father had certainly given a new interpretation to that commandment.

Slamming the screen door behind him, Marsh entered the house. Personally, he intended to keep as much distance as possible between himself and his new neighbor.

Four months was going to seem like an eternity.

Three days after she moved into her grandfather's house, Linnea had her own quarters fixed up just the way she wanted them. She'd chosen to convert the attic into a combination bedroom and office, installing a new air conditioner to ward off excess heat.

It had yet to be used. The day she'd arrived had been the warmest of the month to date. Ever since, the weather had been near perfect. Although that was supposed to change today, with highs predicted above ninety degrees, this morning she still had all the windows open. A fresh, clean-smelling breeze wafted through the upper level of her house, bringing with it the distinctive aroma of freshly cut grass.

Only two stations came in well on her small, battery-powered radio, given the mountainous surroundings. One played nothing but country music. The other featured golden oldies. Today, in honor of the predicted weather, a disc jockey named Caribou Jack was offering a heat-wave medley.

Linnea smiled as Otis Redding sang, imagining docks by cool water. Even the thought of boardwalks was pleasant, but the image of a city rooftop did nothing for her. She'd been there and done that, stood "up on the roof" and looked down on a bustling metropolis far below. What engulfed anyone at that height was not relief from the heat but a noxious mixture rising from the streets. Smog, for lack of a better word.

There were no tall buildings in this part of the world, Linnea thought as she made up the Victorian-era bed she'd found in one of the downstairs bedrooms. Unless she wanted to count lighthouses, and those were on the coast, more than an hour's drive away.

In another month she knew she'd be glad that heat rose, but for now she appreciated the cooling drafts. By the time she left Austin's Crossing, it would be winter, with cold winds whipping through the eaves. She found, to her surprise, that she was actually looking forward to living there when the snow began to fly.

Singing along with the next tune, she ran a feather duster over the treasures she'd unearthed in the rest of the house and in what Cassie had called the barn chamber. Her clothes hung in a standing closet. One corner held a huge wire birdcage with a stuffed parrot in it. Two trunks would serve to store the other possessions she'd sent for from Albany.

The front windows filled up most of the space on that wall because the roof slanted down sharply on either side of them. Linnea was using an old cedar hope chest as a window seat. When she flicked the feather duster in that direction, she moved close enough to the white lace curtains to take a peek out. She was just in time to see Marshall Austin pass by on his way to the store.

Drat.

She needed another extension cord and one or two other items, but she'd meant to buy them while Emma was in charge of the market. She'd carefully avoided Marsh Austin since those two memorable run-ins the first day.

Coward.

So he rattled her? So what? And there was one matter she did need to discuss with him.

"No time like the present," she muttered.

After a quick check in the mirror, to make sure she didn't have smudges on her cheeks or cobwebs in her hair, she hurried downstairs and out of the house, then walked the short distance to Austin's Crossing Market at a studiously sedate pace.

Marsh was working behind the tiny meat counter this time, an apron covering his torso and a blood-stained meat cleaver in one hand. The sight took her aback for a moment.

"Good thing I've been assured that you're harmless," she said, grinning.

"I wouldn't be so sure about that."

Her smile faded and for a moment panic flared. Then she got her wayward imagination under control again. She'd heard enough about him from Jen and Cassie to know he was not a danger to anyone.

He just didn't like her.

"Could we please have a civilized conversation?" she asked. "Ten minutes?"

A shrug answered her. He went back to cutting steaks and roasts out of a large piece of meat.

"I would like to know why you wanted to buy my house."

"I'm sure you would." The cleaver came down hard.

"I can always ask Jen or Cassie."

He stopped cutting and carefully set the sharp blade aside. His hands gripped the edge of the counter, and Linnea had the uneasy notion that he was wishing he could wrap them around her throat.

"Don't even think about trying to turn my family against me, lady, or you'll regret it."

"Has anyone ever told you you're paranoid? I have no intention of causing trouble. That's why I'm here. I want my answers directly from you."

"You just threatened to go behind my back."

"I did not . . . threaten." She threw her hands up in defeat. "Oh, what's the use?"

His voice caught up with her before she could take more than a few steps toward the door. "I needed more room for the dogs."

She returned slowly and frowned at him over the top of the glass case. Only his head and shoulders were visible from that angle and his expression was not encouraging.

"I don't have much of a yard."

"I meant to tear down the house and outbuildings and fence in the entire lot."

Recoiling as if she'd been slapped, Linnea gasped. "How could you even think about destroying that lovely old—"

"Wreck? Take off the rose-colored glasses, Linnea."

"I know it needs work."

"Good. And for the record, I hope you succeed."

"Really?" He'd managed to surprise her. Again.

"Sure." He shrugged. "The sooner you finish playing interior decorator, the sooner you'll leave."

"Charming."

"Look, I've accepted that you don't want to sell to me, but I have no reason to want you to fail. Your decision is inconvenient for me, but not enough to make me want to cause you trouble."

"I didn't think it was."

"You should have. It should have occurred to you that I might try to force you out. Scare you into selling. Hell, lady. I know you're afraid of the dogs."

"What were you planning to do, turn them loose in the middle of the night?"

"Don't tempt me."

"They're friendly, remember? Besides, I have sense enough to stay inside at night."

A wicked gleam sparked in his eyes. "The lock on your front door is a joke. Anyone could break in. Anytime. Or climb through one of your windows."

"Now who's threatening?"

And why did she feel invigorated by the growing

tension between them? Why was she imagining him slipping into her house some dark night, slipping into her bedroom, slipping into—

Hot color flooded her face, provoking a thoughtful look from her nemesis.

"Enough of this neighborly chitchat," he said. "I have work to do."

"I came in for an extension cord . . . and a truce."

"Extension cords are in aisle three."

"And the truce?"

"The dead-bolt locks are about a foot away from the electrical supplies, on your right."

As he headed for the embankment at the back of his property, Marsh avoided looking at the Dennison house. She'd been living next door to him for two weeks now.

He'd caught sight of her once or twice since their conversation in the store. More in evidence had been the multitude of utility workers, contractors, and delivery vans arriving and departing. More traffic than the sleepy little burg of Austin's Crossing had seen in years.

At the stone fireplace they used for cookouts, Marsh stopped to survey the scene on the riverbank below. The path down was steep and there was little of what they called their beach left. The water was slowly eroding the land away. In time, even the fireplace would collapse and fall over the edge.

Not today, though.

Right now, in high summer, the river was sluggish and low. Marsh scrambled down, taking care with his footing, until he reached the small, beached boat his sister had claimed for her own. It had a gaping hole in one side and was firmly wedged in among the rocks along the riverbank. Across the bow, Cassie had painted THINK OR SWIM.

Nobody knew where the craft had come from, but when it became obvious no one else wanted it, Cassie had made it into her own private clubhouse. Marsh rapped lightly on the door of the tiny cabin.

"Come on in, Linnea," his sister called.

Marsh's hand clenched into a fist. "It's not Linnea."

"You can come in anyway," Cassie called back.

When he lifted the latch, the door creaked open to reveal a rough wooden bench and a tattered rug on the floor. A rickety bookcase held several plastic-wrapped packages, a battery-powered lantern, and a small picnic cooler.

"Hi, big brother," Cassie said. She had been reading a book while curled up on top of her folded sleeping bag, which padded one end of the bench. She left it in the clubhouse all summer long, although as far as Marsh knew she'd yet to work up enough nerve to camp out here alone overnight.

"You were expecting Linnea, short stuff?"

Cassie shrugged. "Maybe. She's been here once."

"You showed her your secret clubhouse?" That surprised him. Disturbed him too. Denise Dennison's daughter was not the sort of person he wanted his sister to hang out with.

"Uh-huh," Cassie answered. "Know what? Linnea almost had a tree house once. She told me she used to live in this house that had this great big tree out in front. When she was about my age, she wanted to build a tree house in it, and she told her mother what she wanted to do, but she said it would cost too much. So Linnea started saving up her allowance to buy the materials, but before she could save enough, the town came and cut the tree down, because its roots were bowing up the sidewalk. And then her mother made her put all the money she'd saved into a savings bond."

"Bummer," Marsh said, though the last thing he wanted to do was sympathize over something that had happened between Denise and Linnea. "So, Cass— have you been seeing a lot of our new neighbor?"

"Sure. She's still a little spooked by the dogs, but otherwise she's cool."

Without further prompting, Cassie expanded on the subject, chattering away about Linnea to such an extent that Marsh began to feel alarm. He didn't want his sister hurt when the woman left. Enough people in her life had already let her down.

"She wants me to help her with a 3-D jigsaw puzzle," Cassie announced.

A sense of guilt tweaked Marsh. Puzzles were something he and Cassie had done together in the past, but he hadn't had much time for play lately.

Maybe he'd better find some.

"She's got it set up in the attic," Cassie went on. "That's where she's sleeping. She says she picked the attic for her bedroom because she likes to listen to the sound of rain on the roof when she's lying in bed."

The image was vivid, but Marsh forced it away.

"Aunt Jen sent me down to tell you she's ready to leave to go shopping. She says the two of you are going to look for clothes for school."

"Do I have to go? School's a long way off."

"Classes start in another month."

"I'm in the middle of my book."

"It'll keep. Jen is missing one of her regular afternoons at the community center for this. The least you can do is finish reading your story later."

"Oh, all right." Cassie marked her place carefully. "What are you reading?"

"It's this cool book about the Underground Railroad. You know. Abolitionists smuggling slaves out of the South and into Canada. Did you know it used to run right through Jefferson County?"

"Guess I heard something like that," Marsh said, not much interested.

"Wouldn't it be great if we could find a hidden station here?"

"You mean a tunnel leading down to the river from a secret room in our cellar?" He knew how Cassie's imagination worked.

"Yeah! Wouldn't that be cool?"

"Cool," he agreed, confident there were no hidden rooms or tunnels. If there had ever been any such hiding places in the house, he'd have known.

He and Cassie left the boat and started back up the hill. At the top, his sister paused to look at the house next door. "Maybe Linnea would let me search her cellar too."

Not what he wanted to hear. "Maybe you shouldn't bother her, Cassie. She has a lot of work to do on that house."

"Oh, it's okay. Linnea says I can come over anytime."

He tried again. "I doubt she's interested in local history."

"Yes she is." Cassie's earnest expression tore at his heart. "She's been asking all kinds of questions about Austin's Crossing. Her family used to live here, you know."

Marsh took the blow without showing any reaction, but it sent him reeling all the same. Damn. That was all he needed. Linnea Bryan stirring up the townspeople's long memories with questions about her mother.

Bad enough she was setting Cassie up for a fall.

Now she might set the whole town talking again, as well.

He seriously thought about forbidding Cassie to spend any more time with their new neighbor, but he knew that wasn't wise. She'd only rebel against his authority and end up angry at him. He didn't want that.

He had a legitimate concern, he told himself. If Cassie got too attached to Linnea, she'd be devastated when the woman left town.

Four months.

Long enough to do a lot of harm.

There was no way to avoid having another talk with Linnea Bryan, he decided. He'd keep it short, just get the message across that he didn't approve of her associating with Cassie.

Maybe he could think of a way to put an end to her nosy poking around too.

Did she know about her mother and his father? Marsh didn't think so, and that was the way he wanted to keep it. It would be better for everyone if Linnea never found out what her mother had done.

Protective instincts again? he asked himself.

Marsh was frowning as he watched Jen and Cassie drive off on their shopping trip. Jen liked Linnea. Cassie adored her. And damned if now and again he didn't find himself admiring the woman too.

Big mistake. He could not afford to let his guard down. She was Denise's daughter. That made her unpredictable . . . and dangerous.

He ought to stay away from her.

He told himself that his responsibilities to his family made that impossible.

Glancing at his watch, he saw he had more than an hour until he was due to relieve Emma. There seemed no point in putting off an unpleasant task. He left his own yard and headed for Linnea's back door.

He knocked, but with all the noise inside—a sander, from the sound of it—he knew she couldn't hear him. When he discovered the door wasn't locked, he let himself in.

He was in the kitchen, wondering why he was so irritated that she'd ignored his warning about the danger of potential intruders, when he heard her cry out in alarm.

Seconds later a tremendous crash echoed through the house.

FOUR

Coughing, her eyes tearing, Linnea felt her way blindly, aiming for the nearest exit and a breath of fresh air. Her ears were ringing, too, but not loudly enough to mask the sound of heavy footsteps.

The last thing she expected, or wanted, was company, and even before Marsh called out her name, concern obvious in his deep voice, she had a premonition that he was her uninvited visitor. Who else could it be? The way her luck had been running all day, the only other possibility was Jason from all those *Friday the 13th* movies.

With just a second to prepare herself, Linnea had to settle for squinting belligerently at him when he shoved aside the sheet she'd hung across the archway between the living room and dining room. It was supposed to keep the dust she raised from drifting throughout the house, but it wasn't any barrier at all to a large male person.

He came to an abrupt halt, scanned her long enough to assure himself she was relatively unscathed, then gave a low whistle. "Got yourself a bit of a plaster disaster," he observed in that irritating laconic drawl.

Northerners, she decided, should not be allowed to drawl. It had much too disconcerting an effect.

"Can't fix up till you tear down first," she shot back.

"Well, you're certainly doing that."

Linnea refused to admit, especially to Marsh Austin, that she was a total washout as a handyperson. She also fought a completely unacceptable urge to fling herself into his arms and sob her heart out against his broad chest. She wasn't hurt, just frustrated. There was no need to go to pieces.

Deliberately, she turned her back on him.

The living room looked like a bomb had gone off.

A small one, she told herself, but the thought did little to cheer her up.

The dropcloth she'd put down over the wide oak floorboards was coated with fine white powder, as she'd expected when she'd taken the sander to the plaster ceiling. What she hadn't counted on was that the vibrations would jar bigger things loose. In addition to the dust, there were large chunks of ceiling lying there. And the light fixture.

She swallowed hard before she looked up.

Great gaping sections of the ugly surface once hidden by the plaster were now exposed. She didn't have a clue how to fix the holes. The books she'd taken out of the local library had only covered the basics. None too well, either, to judge by the series of mishaps that had preceded this one.

Blinking rapidly, she turned back to Marsh. "Never did care for that ugly old chandelier."

"Not worth crying about," he agreed.

She started to wipe her eyes but he stopped her, catching both of her hands in his. "Don't. You'll get plaster dust in them."

"It's just the dust that's irritating them now," she said. "I'm not the type of woman who cries over minor setbacks like this one."

He gave her a look of patent disbelief, then kept hold of her hands and hauled her after him out of the room. He took her by way of the front hall but turned left, heading back to the kitchen and out through the utility room to reach the great outdoors.

"The front porch was closer," she grumbled as she broke free of his grip at last and filled her lungs with blessedly fresh, sweet air.

"You don't want folks to think I'm courting you, do you?"

"What?"

Her utter astonishment faded when she realized he couldn't be serious. She was standing there, literally covered with plaster dust, her hair no doubt sticking out in ghastly spikes. She couldn't imagine a more unlikely object for anyone's romantic interest. If Marsh were to kiss her now, he'd end up looking like a mime in whiteface.

The image of clownish makeup on Marsh's stern features produced an unexpected giggle. Then she started to chuckle. A moment later the sound had turned into a full-fledged laugh. More tears streamed down her face, probably smearing the plaster. The knowledge that she'd have the devil of a time getting herself cleaned up only made her whoop louder.

It felt wonderful. Liberating.

And best of all, Marsh was quickly infected by her mirth. He had more self-control than she, but even he couldn't hold back a broad grin.

He folded his arms across his chest and waited for her to settle down. It took a solid five minutes and she was still gasping a bit and had to cling to his forearm for support before she could manage to get a grip on the hilarity. She sucked in a deep, calming breath and finally, with a last squeak, subsided.

"Done?"

She nodded, reluctant to trust her voice just yet. It wouldn't take much to set her off again.

"Too bad we don't still have an old well here in the dooryard. You could do with sluicing down."

Dooryard. Barn Chamber. Mud Room. She was learning an entirely new vocabulary here. Were there really all that many differences between the city mouse and the country mouse?

"I'll sluice down in the kitchen, thank you. And just what was with that crack about courting? Are there some hidden meanings involved in using the front door?"

Linnea brushed past him into the house, ignoring another tingle of awareness as they touched. She ought to be getting used to that by now. It happened every time they made any physical contact with each other, no matter how slight.

She grabbed a dish towel and headed for the sink. There didn't seem to be much point in doing more than a minimal cleanup, not when she had all that debris to clear away in the front room. Besides, now that Marsh had already seen her at her worst, anything was an improvement.

Irritated that she was even tempted to fuss for his sake, Linnea gave herself a stern lecture. She did not want to encourage his interest. Even if she was the type for flings, he'd just very properly reminded her what a small town this was. Why, they probably still had shotgun weddings in these parts!

"Folks around here don't use the front door much," he said. "If you're friendly, neighbors come 'round to the back."

It was a real pity that she was starting to like him, Linnea thought as she scrubbed at the worst of the plaster. She'd probably even miss him when she left Austin's Crossing for good. Thoroughly annoyed by that thought, she spoke without first thinking her words through.

"The back door? In most civilized places that would be the tradesmen's entrance."

As soon as she'd uttered the taunting words, she regretted them. He'd already categorized her as a city-bred snob. Now she'd gone and reinforced that wrongheaded notion.

His eyes narrowed as her barb hit home. His regional twang became even more pronounced when he answered, as if he used it as a self-defense mechanism. "Front's for funerals. Weddings. Formal occasions." He paused for a beat. "Single fella comes knocking at the front, that's a clue right off you ought to either send him packing or agree to marry him."

"Fella comes knocking at the back," she shot back, "folks might think he's up to no good, maybe has something to hide."

The flicker of strong emotion in his eyes astonished her. Pain? No, it couldn't be. He was just baiting her, stringing her along. Wasn't he? Suddenly she wished she could be certain. For all she knew, he was telling her the simple truth, albeit laid on in that exaggerated accent.

Even though they rubbed each other the wrong way more often than not, Marsh Austin had struck her early on as the honest, straightforward type. Maybe too honest, but at least she usually felt she knew where she stood with him.

"Most folks around here don't have much need for a front door at all," he continued. "Come winter we stuff insulation between it and the storm door and slap a heavy sheet of plastic on the outside. Helps keep the cold out."

"Charming."

"Works."

"Does it keep out unwanted visitors as well?"

"It gets around when someone doesn't want company." He shrugged. "Folks stay away on their own."

"Ah, the taciturn New Englander."

Abruptly both his expression and his voice

changed. The drawl was gone. So was the easy, teasing demeanor. "It's called respecting another person's privacy. We're pretty good at it here. You'd do well to learn the same trick."

"You sure do get testy easily." Linnea was feeling a little put-upon herself. "Did you come over here for a reason?"

For a moment he hesitated, showing what she was sure was an uncharacteristic uncertainty. "Just being neighborly," he finally said.

She heard the irony in his voice, but before she could react he startled her with an offer.

"Could you use an assistant?" he asked, gesturing toward the living room. A plaster cloud still hung in the air, like low fog on a sunny day. "I work cheap."

Linnea bit off her automatic refusal just in time. She couldn't read his enigmatic expression. Humble didn't come into it, but for some reason she felt he really wanted her to accept his offer.

Why?

Marsh already had two jobs that she knew of, at the store and with the dogs. She tried to remember if her conversations with Cassie had indicated that the family had to live frugally to make ends meet. What if Marsh Austin needed work? A third job to tide him over until sledding season?

That seemed the likely answer to his presence, with cap figuratively in hand. The dogs couldn't be bringing in any money at this time of year and the store wasn't exactly an inner-city 7-Eleven.

He had Cassie to support. It took a lot just to

clothe a growing girl. And then there was his aunt Jen. Jen did some kind of part-time work at home, using a computer, but her medical expenses had to be substantial and insurance only went so far. That state-of-the-art wheelchair wasn't cheap. Neither were her thrice-weekly sessions of physical therapy in New Portsmouth. Or the specially equipped van she drove with hand controls.

Linnea's gaze strayed to Marsh's leg. She still didn't know what had caused his limp, though by now she'd guessed it had been a while since he'd been injured. She'd started at least a dozen times to ask Cassie or Jen for details, but each time she'd stopped, feeling like a snoop going behind Marsh's back. She hadn't stopped wondering, though. Sometimes there was barely a trace of a limp when he walked. At others she sensed he was in considerable pain.

"Just spit it out," he said irritably. "If you aren't interested, say so."

His words made her aware she'd been standing there, wiping her hands on the towel, speculating about things that were none of her business, for an unpardonably long time.

"I could use some help," she said carefully. "I guess that's pretty obvious."

There. She'd made an effort. What more could he ask?

"Fine," he said. "I have to get to the store now, but I'll be back tomorrow and clean up that mess in the living room."

"I can handle the cleanup myself. I'm no fragile

flower, Marsh." She hesitated. In some ways she might be in better shape physically than he was. "Look, I know you probably won't think it's any of my business, but if I'm going to hire you, then I need to know how bad that leg of yours is. Is it likely to give out on you? Can you do heavy lifting? Can you—"

His look stopped her midway through the third question, before she could ask him what she really wanted to know—how he'd injured himself in the first place.

"Let's clear up some confusion here," he said. "You aren't hiring me. I don't expect to be paid. I'm offering to help as a neighbor. Out of the goodness of my heart."

Embarrassed, she winced at the sarcasm that imbued the last part of that little speech and said the first thing that came to mind.

"But you don't even want me here."

Linnea felt herself blushing and wished she could sink through the floor. Or hide in the hole in her living-room ceiling.

"Never mind," she went on. "I understand. The sooner the renovations are done, the sooner I'll be gone."

Hadn't he already told her that? She was an idiot to think anything had changed.

"Yeah," he said, but his voice lacked conviction.

The way he was glowering at her roused her suspicions all over again. If he didn't expect to be paid and he didn't like her, why offer to do something that would necessitate spending a good deal of his free time with her? She'd be gone soon enough without his help. There was no need to make such a sacrifice.

On the other hand, she could certainly use the help. She was the first to admit she was out of her depth here. Why not accept, even if it hadn't been the most gracious of offers?

"You are an aggravating man," she told him.

He had her confused on every level. Physical. Emotional. Even practical. In all of those areas he was exerting an undeniable pull . . . and at the same time he was pushing her away.

"It's a gift. Look, Linnea, the offer was sincerely meant. In this town, people help each other out. If you feel you owe me for that, then maybe you can do a favor for me sometime."

Possibilities hung between them, unspoken. Linnea wasn't certain if he failed to voice them because he couldn't think of anything specific, or because he could. The concept of her doing favors for him, to pay off her debt to him, sure put a few ideas into *her* mind. Some of them were the sort that should never be spoken aloud.

"I suppose I could have you and Jen and Cassie over for dinner," she said quickly. That sounded both safe and neighborly.

"You cook?"

Those two words, uttered in astonishment, sparked her temper once again. Aggravating? The word didn't begin to describe how he affected her.

Only the fact that she spotted a devilish gleam in those maple-syrup eyes of his kept her in control of herself. She repressed the urge to haul off and smack him on the arm for his wisecrack and instead made her voice saccharine sweet.

"Guess you'll have to take a chance and find out," she all but simpered at him.

"Guess I will." The drawl was back.

Then Marsh tipped an imaginary hat and sauntered out her back door.

All the way to the store, Marsh tried to figure out what had just happened. He'd gone over to the Dennison house to warn Linnea to stay away from Cassie. He'd never intended to volunteer to help her with her renovations.

He'd been scared for her when he'd heard that crash, and relieved to find her still in one piece.

And astonished to discover that a woman covered in plaster dust could still look sexy.

She'd charmed him when she'd been able to laugh at herself. In the span of a few seconds he'd gone from wanting to protect her, to wanting to strangle her, to wanting, very badly, to make passionate love to her.

Marsh shook his head, trying to dislodge Linnea from his mind, and took the steps up to the market door two at a time. Once Emma had gone back to her apartment, though, images of Linnea returned to haunt him. Linnea in her city clothes. Linnea in tight jeans. Linnea covered with plaster. Linnea in nothing at all.

Whether he was doing the accounts or dusting the

shelves or checking inventory, she kept intruding. Finally he gave up and let thoughts of her flow freely.

Okay. He was attracted to her, male to female. And unless he'd completely lost his instincts about such things, she was equally attracted to him. He grinned suddenly. She didn't like it any more than he did.

Three and a half months were left of her four. Just about right for a brief, hot affair.

Whoa! Denise's daughter, he reminded himself. Remember what happened to your own father.

Marsh also belatedly remembered that he'd gone over to Linnea's meaning to drive a wedge between her and Cassie. His smile faded fast. His sister's name had come up only once, when Linnea had included her in that unexpected invitation to dinner.

How to keep them apart—that was his dilemma. An obvious solution presented itself, one he'd already implemented, though not intentionally.

The more he considered the possibilities, the more he was convinced that his initial determination to stay away from Linnea Bryan had been a mistake. That had left her with too much time to fraternize with Cassie and Jen. Instead, he needed to keep her too busy with him to have time for anyone else.

Justification for interfering with Cassie's budding friendship wasn't hard to come up with. Linnea wouldn't stick around any more than Denise had. The less Cassie saw of her, the less she'd be hurt.

By the same token, since *he* wasn't a little girl with

tender feelings, there was no reason he couldn't enjoy Linnea's company.

When he looked at the situation coolly and logically, he found no reason at all not to act on the attraction between himself and Linnea Bryan. He was pretty sure that given a choice, she'd prefer his company to that of a child. He'd help her with the house and keep her so busy with that, and in bed, that she'd have no time left over to spend with anyone else. Or to dig into her family's past.

Sounded like a plan to him.

The phone rang just as Linnea disposed of the last of the mess from the living room. She'd felt compelled to clean up the disaster area. Not because Marsh Austin had wanted her to leave it for him, she assured herself, but just because she hated to wake up to unfinished projects when she didn't have to.

She knew who would be on the other end of the line even before she answered. It was after nine at night, too late for any of the good citizens of Austin's Crossing to be bothering their neighbors. They were scrupulous about things like that. They also went to bed with the chickens.

"Hello, Mother," she said. It was three hours earlier in California. Her mother was probably still at the office.

Denise's clipped tones came through loud and clear, and Linnea held the receiver away from her ear. She didn't bother to listen for the first ten minutes or so. Only when she heard the words *take his offer* did she snap to attention.

"What? Why?"

"Because you don't want to stay there any longer than you have to. Believe me, Linnea, there's nothing for you in Austin's Crossing."

Where had she heard *that* before? For a moment she wondered if Marsh had been talking to her mother. Then she dismissed the thought as pure paranoia. No one was conspiring against her. This was just one more instance of Denise Dennison Bryan trying to manipulate her only child's behavior.

"So I should sell for a song to Marsh Austin?" she asked. "Let him tear down the house? Then eat canned beans until I find another job?"

"You can come work for me. You know that."

"No, Mother, I can't." They'd gone around and around on that idea more times than she wanted to count.

Distance allowed them to carry on a civilized, if not entirely harmonious, conversation. When they were in the same room with each other, the record for an absence of friction was less than two hours.

"I suppose little Marsh must be all grown up by now," Denise remarked.

"You could say that." Was he ever!

"Did he tell you I used to be his baby-sitter?"

Linnea tried to imagine it and couldn't. She wasn't sure which was harder to visualize, the man next door as a small child or her mother as a teenager. "He hasn't mentioned you at all."

"Just like his father, I'll bet." Denise's laugh sounded strained. "You watch yourself. Those strong, silent types can be dangerous."

Frowning, Linnea didn't respond to that rather ambiguous comment, didn't know how to, though her curiosity was definitely piqued. "I kind of like it here," she said instead. "It's peaceful."

"Dead."

A contradiction, surely. Unless Denise was implying that the Austin men were vampires. Linnea smiled at the thought. She wouldn't mind letting Marsh Austin nibble on her neck.

"Quiet," she said aloud.

"Dull," her mother countered. "Darling, you're being foolish. If you insist on providing yourself with enough money to tide you over, why not sell that ridiculous car? You know my friend Bernie would give you a good price."

"Never!" The suggestion pushed all thought of Marsh out of Linnea's mind.

"Now, darling—"

"This is another argument we've had before," Linnea cut in. Denise just didn't get it. She talked about "boys and their toys" in regard to selling the car to good old Bernie, the Connecticut Gold Coast millionaire who'd been her friend for twenty years, but she'd never understand what her daughter saw in the Mustang.

"What self-respecting businesswoman owns a pony car?" Denise asked. "For heaven's sake, Linnea, that model isn't even as high-powered as the later ones. I don't know why you . . ."

Linnea blocked out her mother's familiar litany.

How could she explain a purely emotional aberration? Her attachment to the car didn't make sense to Linnea, either, though she understood perfectly the sequence of events that had led her to buy it. It had been several years ago. She'd been talking to a friend, confessing that she no longer expected to be swept off her feet by a knight in shining armor on his trusty charger. Her friend, who had been just as disillusioned as Linnea, had quipped, "Not even a Dodge Charger." A week later, Linnea had spotted the Mustang, sporting a "For Sale" sign. She'd thought to herself, Close enough.

Buying the car hadn't been a rational act, but that hadn't mattered then and it didn't now. She'd made, she supposed, a symbolic gesture, and had never regretted it. The car was fun to own and fun to drive . . . and it somehow represented freedom to her. She didn't need a knight in shining armor or even a sunset. She could make her own dreams come true. She had her own faithful steed.

Or so she'd thought until the corporate downsizing.

Linnea frowned, but only until she remembered that the car had brought her here to Austin's Crossing, to new dreams. To a decision that was, perhaps, equally irrational, but about which she had not a single regret. She would fix up this grand old house. She might even live in it for a while afterward, just to enjoy the fruits of her labor.

"Mother," she said aloud, interrupting the spate of words. "I assure you that I am still practical enough to sell the Mustang if I have to, if that's the only way to avoid starvation, for example, but short of being in such dire straits, there is no way I'm going to part with it."

A clicking sound cut into Denise's retort. "I've got another call coming in," her mother said. "Think again about getting rid of that car, Linnea. And think about my offer of a job again too. Seriously, this time. You could do worse than work for my company."

"I don't think so, Mother."

"I swear, you're getting more like your father every day." With that parting shot, Denise Dennison Bryan hung up on her unsatisfactory daughter.

"I love you, too, Mom," Linnea said as she quietly cradled the phone.

She thought about calling her father, but conversations with Larry Bryan were even more difficult than those with Denise. He was an artist who preferred solitude. Years earlier he'd given up a lucrative career in finance—and his wife and baby daughter—to follow his muse.

Linnea saw him once or twice a year, spoke with him on the phone two or three times more, and for months on end forgot she even had a father. He hadn't been there for her when she was growing up. She didn't miss him now.

Family.

Such a strange concept, she mused. Just being in this house, where generations of Dennisons had lived and died, made her aware of all the word had once meant. It sparked her curiosity too. Denise's few comments just now had doubled the sum total of all she'd ever said to Linnea about growing up in Austin's Crossing. She'd been seventeen when she left, if Linnea remembered right.

Denise had been Marsh Austin's baby-sitter.

The mind boggled.

Linnea had asked the lawyer why her grandfather had left his house to her rather than to her mother. The lawyer hadn't known, but Linnea was sure someone must. Not Cassie. Too young. Not Jen. Linnea had asked her already and received only vague answers. She'd gotten the impression Jen hadn't liked the neighbor she'd called "Old Man" Dennison much, and that he'd been something of a recluse.

How much did Marsh remember about him?

Tomorrow, she decided, she'd ask. And she'd find out how he'd injured his leg, as well.

Smiling, Linnea headed upstairs for a long, luxurious soak in her grandfather's claw-footed bathtub. She was looking forward to her next meeting with Marsh with intense anticipation, a feeling she hadn't known for a long time.

A feeling, she realized, that she'd missed.

FIVE

"My mother told me to say hi to little Marsh," Linnea said by way of greeting the next morning.

Taken aback, Marsh automatically assumed the guarded, almost surly facade he'd perfected for police work. "Why would she say that?" he asked.

The coffee mug Linnea was holding out to him suddenly wasn't as steady as it had been when he first walked in. She hastily placed it on the scarred Formica surface of the kitchen table. With a wariness that was almost palpable, she answered him. "Because she used to be your baby-sitter?"

"Told you that, did she?"

"Yes. On the phone. Last night. What's with you this morning, Marsh? Change your mind about helping me?" She retreated to the other side of the table and picked up her own mug of coffee, taking a sip as she waited for his answer.

"I'm here, aren't I?"

But things definitely weren't going the way he'd anticipated. He picked up the mug of coffee she'd apparently made for him and downed a third of the fragrant, steaming brew in one gulp. At least she made good coffee, strong and black, just the way he liked it.

For the moment all thoughts of seducing Linnea Bryan had fled. Denise had come between them. "So, how is your mother these days?" he asked.

And how much did she tell you?

"Rich," Linnea said bluntly. "I suppose you were too young to know what she was really like when she lived here, but I'm sure she's always been ambitious. She managed to achieve all her career goals, in spite of being saddled with a child."

"You sound bitter. She treated me well enough when she took care of me." Only in leaving had she hurt him.

A tinge of pink colored Linnea's cheeks. Embarrassment? Anger? Marsh couldn't tell.

"I hope I'm not destroying any childhood illusions," she said, "but my mother is a high-powered businesswoman these days. Her main interest is in the bottom line. No emotions are allowed to interfere with her life. I doubt you'd like her much. I don't myself."

"You don't like your own mother?" This, he had not expected. He frowned as he watched his neighbor polish off her coffee, then abruptly stand and stalk toward the sink.

She made a production of rinsing out her mug. "Oh, don't get me wrong. I don't hate her. In fact, I love her. I just don't like her much. Is that so hard to believe? Did you always get along with *your* mother?"

"Not always, but I did like her."

Except, of course, for the brief period when he'd hated her for leaving him behind. He had no intention of sharing that with Linnea, though. He could see it now, running through a chronology of his life for her benefit. Abandoned at five by baby-sitter and father. Left fatherless by his dad's death when he was seven. Deserted by his mother at fourteen so she could remarry and go away with her second husband.

The only constant had been that he'd continued to live next door, in his grandparents' house, until he was seventeen. First he'd been surrounded by family, both his parents and his father's parents, then he and his mother had stayed on with his grandparents, who'd been as outraged by his father's actions as Marsh's mother had been. Finally there had just been Gram and Gramps. He'd left them behind, along with everyone else in Austin's Crossing, the moment he'd been accepted as a criminal-justice major by the University of Maine.

"Are either of your parents still living?" Linnea asked.

He drained his own mug, giving himself time to decide how much to tell her. It seemed obvious she didn't know about their parents' shared past.

"No," he said at last.

He didn't elaborate. He didn't even like to remember that by the time his mother had returned to Austin's Crossing, pregnant with Cassie and on the outs with her second husband, he'd coldly scorned her overtures. He'd used every excuse in the book to avoid spending time with her on his visits home, even after it was clear she and his new sister were back for good.

He'd had a life, a career, in Boston by then. When he did get back to Maine, he had to spend most of his vacation time working the dogs, helping out the old folks. Or so he told himself. Only after his grandparents were dead and Aunt Jen was in a wheelchair had he come home for an extended stay. He'd thought about moving back then. Instead he'd hired people to help Jen and his mother with the sled-dog business, using the excuse that he had his own obligations in the city, both professional and personal.

And then he'd been shot in the line of duty. Once again his mother had asked him to come home. Once again he'd refused, even though he'd seen how much her health was failing.

A sudden, shocking thought struck Marsh. Denise must have aged, just as his mother had. He kept thinking of her as a vivacious teenage girl, but she was nearly Jen's age.

"Do you have a recent picture of your mother?" he asked abruptly.

Startled, Linnea began to say something, then obviously thought better of it. She turned to her purse, lying on the kitchen counter, and took out her wallet. Flipping to the photo section, she showed him a picture of a sophisticated, hard-eyed woman who looked nothing like the baby-sitter Marsh remembered.

"That's Denise?"

Linnea shrugged. "That's a copy of the portrait photo that hangs in the lobby of her company. She hired one of those glamour photographers to get the image right . . . and take about ten years off her appearance. I don't have any candid shots. She won't allow them."

Marsh had pictures of his mother. Too many showing her frailty, her steadily deteriorating health. He'd ignored her decline, and then it had been too late. Jen had phoned to tell him his mother had died.

With soul-searing honesty, Marsh faced the truth at last. He'd been punishing his mother for abandoning him. For being more like Denise Dennison than he'd ever dared admit when she was alive.

"Marsh?" Linnea's voice brought him back to the present.

He scowled at her. All these morose thoughts were her doing. Usually he could avoid dwelling on things he couldn't change. It did no good to rehash the past.

"If we're going to get anything accomplished, we'd better get to work," he announced. If he sounded impatient, so be it. "There's that mess in the living room to—"

"Done," she said.

"Then you need to have someone come and take a look at the hole in the ceiling, unless you think you can fix it yourself."

She surprised him by agreeing without any argument, and asking him to recommend someone to do the job.

The rest of the morning was a balancing act.

Marsh alternated between reluctant admiration for what Linnea had already accomplished and irritation that she'd invaded his life at all, stirring up old memories and new desires.

His plan to keep her separated from Cassie hit a snag almost at once. It was obvious from her remarks that she liked his sister every bit as much as Cassie liked her.

By the end of that first session, Marsh conceded partial defeat. The best he'd be able to do, unless he wanted to play the role of grinch, was to try to subtly ensure that the time Linnea and Cassie spent together wasn't entirely unsupervised. He owed that much to Cassie. Who knew what disruptive ideas Linnea might otherwise, even if only inadvertently, plant in the girl's mind?

The second morning got off to an even rockier start. Once again Linnea had coffee waiting. By the time he'd finished his second cup, Marsh was feeling comfortable with her. Too comfortable. The kind of comfortable that made a man think about gathering the whole family together and repeating the experience on a daily basis.

They worked side by side for the next three hours, putting down tile on the bathroom floor. It was a test of endurance, especially when she began to talk about bathtubs.

"I love this old claw-footed model," she confided as they carefully eased tile beneath its legs.

"Weighs a ton," he complained.

"Good thing it isn't big enough for two, then."

She wasn't looking at him when she said it, which was probably just as well. He had a feeling the picture he was seeing with his inner eye was clearly reflected on his face.

"I have a friend who built his own bathtub," she went on. "Tiled interior. Cedar splashboards. I think he was actually trying for a hot tub. Anyway, it's huge. So big that he hardly ever uses it because it takes so much water to fill."

"Is that a California thing?" Marsh heard the irritation in his voice and wished he'd kept his mouth shut, but there was no denying that what he was feeling was envy. He didn't like the thought of anyone but him sharing a bathtub with Linnea.

"It was an Albany, New York, thing. And my friend's wife was fit to be tied when she saw the finished bathtub. She told him he ought to consider going into boatbuilding, and put the water on the outside."

"Your friend is married?"

Linnea paused, a floor tile uplifted, and gave him a sharp look. "My friends, plural, are a married couple. They live in my building. Relatives of theirs are subletting my condo. I don't think I like what you're implying, Marsh."

"Sorry. Think of it as a compliment. You're a good-looking woman. Naturally you'd be involved with a man."

"Not a married man," she assured him. "And you need practice giving compliments."

"Could be."

Could be he was also in way over his head with this woman. Time to pull back and regroup, he decided. She rattled him too much to think straight, and he needed all his wits about him when . . . if . . . he took her to bed.

She might not be just like Denise, but she was dangerous to his peace of mind all the same.

Five days after the morning she and Marsh tiled her bathroom floor, Linnea stood at the window in the Austins' kitchen, peering out at the exercise yard, where Marsh was hard at work training three young dogs. They were hitched to a log, dragging it back and forth in compliance with his commands.

"Beauty and skill," she murmured. She meant Marsh's performance as much as that of the animals.

"Those pups are six months old," Jen told her. "In a couple more months they'll be put with experienced dogs so they can begin to copy what the older animals do in harness. When they're fully trained, they sell for over a thousand dollars each."

"Impressive."

Linnea watched awhile longer, surprised to find she was genuinely curious. She wondered if it had anything to do with the fact that she was getting used to being around Foolish. Thanks to Cassie's pet, she was no longer quite so nervous about the Austins' dogs.

"How can he train the dogs to pull a sled when there's no snow on the ground?"

"Around the first of September we start running teams with the ATV." Jen glanced at Linnea, uncertain if she needed to translate.

"All-terrain vehicle?"

Jen nodded. "Since we don't have enough land, Marsh has to take them out on one of the dirt roads nearby. They'll start off running just a mile or two, since they've had most of the summer off. Then they get so they can run a seven-mile course in about a half hour. Marsh tries to exercise each dog a couple of hours a day, and even though he rotates them on a staggered schedule so that each dog runs three days in a row and then takes a day off, he ends up being out there every day. Cassie's a help, of course, but by the time serious training starts, she'll be in school all day and have homework to take up her time in the evenings."

"Three days on, one day off," Linnea said with a soft chuckle. "Same way I do my workout on my stationary bike."

Jen sighed. "I miss being in on this stage of things. Before my accident I did most of the work with the pups. Now I have to wait until winter just to ride along in the sled."

Before Linnea could comment, Jen waved her off. "Don't mind me. I don't usually give in to feeling sorry for myself. Lord knows I have enough to keep me busy without actually training the dogs. It's just that this has been the family business for so long. Our first Siberian husky was brought here from Alaska by

Benjamin Austin back in 1927. Most of the dogs out there are descended from him."

"Was a sledding accident—"

"Oh, no! Sleds are safe as bicycles. Probably safer. A car did me in. Unfortunately, it was soon after my father died. For a long spell, Marsh's mother had to do most everything for the dogs. Little Cassie would tag along. Helping, she'd say." Jen's smile was both sad and full of fond memories. "But Cassandra wasn't ever really well after Cassie's birth. Had her too late in life. She died two years ago."

"I'm so sorry," Linnea murmured. She went and sat at the kitchen table, next to Jen's wheelchair, and touched one of the older woman's hands in what she hoped was a comforting gesture. "Is Cassie an orphan, then?"

That brought Jen's head up with a snap. "Hah! I wish. Her father never was much for taking responsibility, but after Cassandra died he flat out said he wanted no part of his own daughter. Marsh is her legal guardian now."

"Poor kid." Realizing what she'd said, Linnea blushed. "I didn't mean having Marsh . . . I—"

Gentle laughter stopped her sputtering words, and it was Jen's turn to pat Linnea's hands consolingly. "I know what you meant. I like to think that between Marsh and myself, Cassie still has a whole family." She hesitated. "Cassie doesn't seem . . . unhappy to you, does she?"

"Of course not."

Linnea meant her answer, but second thoughts crowded into her mind as soon as the words were out. Cassie did seem extraordinarily quiet at times. Too self-possessed for a child her age. And Linnea remembered very well what that outward calm had covered up in her own case.

Resentment. Boredom. A tendency to get into trouble, though never too serious, in order to attract her too-busy mother's attention. Even being lectured had been better than being ignored.

But Cassie wasn't ignored. There was love in this house. Linnea forced aside the lingering doubts and changed the subject. "Tell me more about Marsh," she said. "Doesn't that leg of his give him trouble when he works long hours with the dogs?"

"Stiffens up some," Jen admitted, "but no more than it does standing on a ladder scraping clapboards."

Put firmly in her place, Linnea abandoned any thought of pumping Jen for information about how Marsh had gotten hurt. "I need to talk to him about tomorrow," she said, excusing herself. "Looks like we're ready to start painting."

As Linnea left the kitchen and headed for the yard, she wondered if she shouldn't just hire someone to do the work, if she could find the money. Having Marsh help hadn't turned out at all as she'd expected. For one thing, there had been little opportunity to talk. Even though Marsh had been spending a few hours each day doing repairs, after the first two mornings, she'd been inside and he'd been outdoors, up on a ladder, out of reach. Conversation had been next to impossible.

Not that it always went that well when they were in the same room. He became guarded, even evasive, every time she expressed too much interest in him, his limp, or his memories of her mother and grandfather.

That had been her first mistake, she realized now. He'd gotten downright surly when she'd mentioned knowing that her mother had once been his baby-sitter.

He was an enigma. She vacillated between wanting to understand him and fearing she might already know too much for her own peace of mind. That was definitely a lustful gleam that came into his eyes every once in a while. It made her nervous, wondering if he ever intended to act on his interest.

Most of the time he was charming. And he'd certainly sped up the restoration process at her place. With the judicious addition of outside help, mostly friends of the Austins with useful experience, the worst of the damage had been fixed in the downstairs rooms. Even the hole in the living-room ceiling had been repaired and a new light fixture installed. She was almost at the point where she could begin to paint woodwork and hang wallpaper. But although Marsh's attitude toward her in general seemed to have mellowed, Linnea was more wary than ever of the chemistry between them.

The closer she got to him as she crossed the lawn, the more nervous she became.

❖━━━━━❖

Marsh sang softly to the dogs throughout the training session, interrupting the song only to give commands. He was still singing when he retrieved his stethoscope and bent to listen to Nora's heartbeat. The pup promptly tried to lick his hand.

"Do you always sing to them?"

Hoping his embarrassment didn't show, Marsh glanced up at Linnea and admitted that he did. "Some folks talk to their dogs. Some never make a sound, except to issue a command."

"Mush?"

"City girl."

"What did I do now?"

"No self-respecting sled dog would know what the heck you meant by that. They know to start for 'hike' and go right at the command 'gee' and left on 'haw.' "

"And to stop?"

"Whoa."

She ventured a few steps closer, still afraid of the ferocious beasts, he supposed. Probably never would get used to being around them.

He wondered if he'd ever get used to dealing with her.

For a week now Linnea had managed to distract him from his plan to lure her into the nearest bed. He kept catching himself either liking her too much to treat her like some cheap pickup, or so annoyed with her that the last thing on his mind was seduction. Then, at regular intervals, she asked disturbing ques-

tions. Those about her own family alternated with
some about his. He figured the latter were just plain
none of her business.

Then there were her questions about his injury.
The more interest she showed in his leg and how he'd
hurt it, the more he resisted satisfying her curiosity.
Ridiculous reaction, but there it was. Linnea Bryan
seemed to bring out a perverse streak in his character.

"Training session over?" she asked.

"For now. This lady needs work, though. She has
a bad habit of gazing at her partner in harness as she
sprints instead of pulling her weight."

"Puppy love?" Linnea asked, and smiled at his
snort of laughter.

"Whatever it is, she'd better grow out of it or the
older dogs will get after her. They've been known to
nip at another dog if she isn't doing her fair share."

"What are you looking for?" Linnea asked as he
continued his routine check of the dog's health. He'd
finished listening to Nora's heart and was now lifting
each foot in turn.

"Cracks. Cuts. On long races, the dogs wear booties for extra protection."

"If it hurts them—"

"It doesn't." Realizing he'd just snapped at her, he
tried to moderate his tone. "Sorry. Some people over-
react. Yell cruelty to animals when there's no cause.
These are working dogs and they love their job, but
the same way your lips get chapped in cold weather,
their footpads can take a beating. That's why we take

special care of them. What I'm doing here is exactly what a vet does after every race. I go through all the same steps to get the dogs used to being examined."

Aware she was watching him with intense interest, he checked each leg, gently pushing and pulling to make sure there were no strains or sprains. Then he checked Nora's eyes and mouth. "Sticky gums indicate dehydration," he explained.

Lifting the dog's tail to check for signs of diarrhea completed the postexercise ritual. Marsh dug into his pocket for a Fig Newton, which served as both a high-energy snack and a reward, then began the examination procedure all over again with Nicky and Asta. He'd been watching an old *Thin Man* movie on television when the time had come to name these three.

"Want to help with feeding them?" he asked Linnea. That might be a way she could "pay him back" for his work on her house. If she was up to it.

"What do they eat?" She sounded game.

"It's a mixture of dry dog food, raw ground meat, and multivitamin powder. Each dog has an individual dish, just as each one has his own kennel to sleep in. Of course, they usually prefer to sleep outside, especially in the winter. They burrow down into a snowbank and stay snug as can be."

"You've got quite a lot of kennels."

Meaning quite a lot of dogs, he translated, and that convinced him she wasn't as comfortable with them as she wanted him to think. Not by a long shot.

"At first," she went on, "I thought that white

building way over there was part of your operation, too, but that's the old schoolhouse, isn't it?"

"Right. Hasn't been used in years, though."

"Any chance you could buy that lot?"

"Feeling guilty?"

"Only curious."

"Well, you'll appreciate this anyway. The school belongs to the town. To New Portsmouth," he added to be clear. "They use the building to store files and the lot to park trucks in. They'd like to tear the schoolhouse down and sell the land. Know why they can't?"

He'd finished the checkup and began walking toward the kennels, the three pups frolicking at his heels. Linnea followed, but stopped abruptly when she caught sight of several adult dogs headed their way.

"No. Why?" she asked.

"Historical-preservation people got word of the plan. There's no money to restore the schoolhouse, but unless it burns down by accident, there's no way to get rid of it, either."

"I suppose you've considered arson."

"Naw. I'm too law-abiding. The only Marshall in town," he joked.

A slow smile rewarded his attempt at humor. Marsh figured that meant she'd pretty much forgiven him for giving her a hard time that first day at the store.

"You going to help me feed them or not?" He jerked his head toward the approaching pack.

"Not." She looked like she was ready to run again,

but she held her ground long enough to ask one more question. "When are you coming over tomorrow?"

"Morning," he said. "Early."

He was there at dawn, propping the old extension ladder against the back of Linnea's house and climbing up with his bucket of paint. It wasn't until he was all the way to the top and noticed the missing screen and the edge of a white curtain sticking out through the partially open window that he remembered two things.

Linnea had made the attic into her bedroom.

And he'd kidded her, the day she'd come over to the store to buy an extension cord, about how easy it would be for someone to climb in through her windows.

The two thoughts together had an instant effect on his body. Marsh was never sure afterward if that caused the accident or if pure dumb luck came into play, but as he shifted to relieve the sudden strain on his zipper, the ladder jerked.

He had two choices. Fall with it or grab for the windowsill.

As the ladder and paint bucket tumbled toward the ground, Marsh reached for the narrow opening. He caught hold of the bottom edge with both hands, but the impact of his body slamming into the clapboards jarred his weaker arm, and excruciating pain shot from his wrist to his shoulder. That hand slipped, leaving him dangling, holding on for dear life with the other.

SIX

Linnea's brain was in that peculiar realm between sleeping and being awake. She was not quite dreaming. It was more like fantasizing. As a child she had often courted this state, using the time to weave adventures, borrowing the characters from her favorite TV shows and adding a prominent role for herself.

Her mind was occupying itself with a rather outlandish scenario that involved Marsh Austin when she heard the thump. It wasn't loud, just emphatic enough to make her start and open her eyes. She'd overslept, she realized. It was morning.

Another faint sound reached her. At first she thought a bird must have flown against the window on the far side of the attic. She was already getting up to take a look when the next odd noise came—a distinctly human grunt.

Rubbing the sleep from her eyes, Linnea left the bedroom area for the "office" half of the attic and peered blearily toward the source of the sound. She was more puzzled than anything else. The first frisson of alarm didn't surface until she realized that the small dark shape on her windowsill was not a bird.

She'd left her curtains open and the window a few inches up. The morning light revealed a clinging hand.

When a second set of fingers joined the first, Linnea's breath caught in her throat. Impossible as it seemed, someone was out there.

The hands shifted. One got a better grip while the other pushed at the bottom of the window, struggling to lift it higher. If it hadn't been morning, she'd have assumed this was a burglar, and although she still couldn't imagine any other explanation, she crept closer, drawn by the sounds of a muffled curse and heavy breathing.

She knew she ought to go back, grab the bedside phone, and call the police. She didn't think the would-be intruder could raise the window the rest of the way from the outside. That meant she had time to call for help. But a new sound kept her moving forward, a frantic scrabbling. She had a sudden, vivid image of shoes slipping on the clapboards. Her house was not tall by city standards, but a fall from this height to the unforgiving ground could still kill or maim.

The next sound she heard filled her with a new kind of terror. It was Marsh's voice, calling her name.

She ran to the window, spurred on by a growing sense of urgency. One glance was all it took to know she was right to be afraid. Marsh's grip was tenuous, and her backyard, at this point more rocky field than lawn, looked very far away. She saw at once what had happened. He'd been up on the ladder, which now lay broken and useless below. A spreading pool of paint stained the green grass, and in her mind blood super-imposed itself on the paint.

In a panic, Linnea fell to her knees on the faded, flowered carpet and wedged her hands in next to Marsh's. She put her whole body into lifting the window. The only thing keeping him from falling was his grip on the sill, but she couldn't help him until they had room to maneuver.

With excruciating slowness, the glass climbed upward. Linnea went with it.

"Thanks," his muffled voice said.

She kept pushing up on the heavy wooden frame. These old-style windows would stay open an inch or so by themselves, but any higher than that, they required something to keep them from slamming shut. For lack of any other handy prop, Linnea braced the bottom edge on her shoulders. The rim bit into her skin, but she gritted her teeth and held on. It was a miracle Marsh hadn't already fallen.

His dark shape dangled below her, apparently helpless. She was trying to decide what to do next, when he moved. With astonishing upper-body strength, he slowly pulled himself upward.

She slid to one side to give him more room, pressing her back against the window frame but still holding the glass as high as she could. Sweat beaded on his forehead, but with a burst of energy and another grunt, he levered himself high enough to tumble in over the sill. Clutching his left shoulder, he landed at her feet.

The window slammed closed with a crash as Linnea released it to fling herself down onto the floor beside him. "You could have been killed." She looked for blood, but found none. "Are you hurt?"

When she reached for his arm, he flinched away. She couldn't see any injuries, but he was in obvious pain. He closed his eyes, as if to gather strength, then managed to speak.

"I'm sound enough. Just winded."

"Marsh, I'm calling a doctor."

His right hand shot out, catching her forearm, holding her in place. "No doctor. No need. No real harm done."

"You nearly scared *me* to death!"

Slowly, he opened his eyes. Even more slowly, his gaze traveled from her face downward, making her vividly aware that she was wearing only a thin nightgown. Her concern for him had brought her close, leaning over him, even before he'd grabbed her arm. His gaze lingered on her unconfined breasts as they rose and fell in rhythm with her quickened breathing.

The hand holding her gentled until his fingers stroked rather than imprisoned. A heated gleam lit up his dark eyes.

Linnea glared back. "Obviously, you're not seriously hurt."

The moment she started to pull away, his grip

tightened again. One tug brought her sprawling full-length on top of him.

"Marsh!"

That was all she could get out before he covered her mouth with his own and began kissing her with the fervor of a man who'd just come way too close to meeting his Maker.

Resistance lasted approximately three seconds. What he was doing felt far too good and Linnea wasn't into self-denial. She suspected she'd regret giving in later, but at this precise moment nothing mattered more than relaxing and enjoying the feel of his sensual lips and inventive tongue.

The man was a dynamite kisser.

Marsh knew he ought to stop.

This wasn't the time or the place for seduction, but miraculously, the ache in his left arm had faded away. His entire focus centered on other parts of his body. And certain parts of hers.

He didn't stop kissing Linnea. He couldn't.

Instead he gathered her closer and explored the delicious skin of her throat, the texture of her earlobe. He'd have gone further if the faint sound of someone calling her name hadn't penetrated the haze of rapidly building passion.

Abruptly, too abruptly to suit either of them, he released her. "That's Cassie's voice," he whispered hoarsely.

The bemused look faded from Linnea's face as she

sprang to her feet. "I can't remember if I locked the back door."

Marsh could reassure her there. He'd knocked and tried the knob before he'd set up the ladder. At the time he'd been annoyed because he'd guessed the locked door meant Linnea was still asleep, and that meant no morning coffee, no intimate conversation in her cozy, disorganized kitchen.

"Don't worry. It's locked."

His words failed to calm Linnea. "I never sleep this late," she muttered as she made tracks for the other side of the attic. "I promised Cassie she could help me paint woodwork this morning. And then I'm supposed to drive her to the library."

So much for keeping Linnea too busy to spend unsupervised time with Cassie, Marsh thought as he struggled to his feet. Damn, his arm was sore, now that he had nothing to distract him from feeling the pain. He flexed it carefully, assessing the damage. He didn't think he'd done anything more than pull a muscle. Maybe not even that.

From the shadows at the front of the room, he could hear Linnea's continued grumbling. She was dressing, he realized. And when she'd thrown on some clothes, she was going to go down and let his little sister in.

"If Cassie hasn't noticed the ladder," he said quickly, "she won't know I'm here. I can slip out once she's occupied with the woodwork. I don't want her to think—"

"Neither do I! I don't even want *you* to think it."

Marsh stared up at the rafters, uncertain what had just happened between them, besides some great kissing. He had no idea where he stood with Linnea.

There was, however, one thing he did know.

A single taste was not enough.

Soon—very soon—he and Linnea were going to finish what they'd started that morning.

Cassie chattered all the way to the library. Linnea scarcely got a word in edgewise. At first, she didn't have much to say anyway. Her thoughts kept drifting. She heard her young companion as if from a great distance and was scarcely even aware of the presence of two dogs, Foolish and Tatupu, in the backseat of the Mustang.

Preoccupied with the memory of what had happened between her and Marsh only a few hours earlier, Linnea had all she could do to concentrate on her driving. She did *not* want to think about those kisses. She didn't dare. But she couldn't seem to stop dwelling on the delicious feel of his mouth on her skin.

She told herself she was grateful Marsh had slipped out, as promised, while she set Cassie to work painting. Now if she could just manage not to see him again until she'd gotten her self-control back, she'd be fine. Unfortunately, Jen had invited Linnea to eat supper at the Austin house that evening. Marsh was bound to be there.

"We had an author visit our school last year," Cassie announced.

Linnea seized on the new subject. Any distraction in a storm. "What did he write?"

"*She* wrote a mystery. Just one. It isn't even in print anymore, so at first we didn't think she could be a very good writer, but she is. Her name is Felicity Madoc. I read her book. It's cool—all about this spooky old house here in Maine. It has a hidden room in it."

"That's kind of fanciful, isn't it? I mean, in a castle, maybe. But how many people have secret rooms in their homes?"

"What about the Underground Railroad?"

"What about it?"

Cassie lowered her voice conspiratorially. "It used to run right through here."

Uncertain what to say to that, Linnea asked about the speaker instead. She had to keep her mind off Marsh's mouth. "So what did this mystery writer talk to your class about?"

"How to write stories. She said that writing a story is like baking a cake. You take certain ingredients and you mix them together. There's flour, shortening, eggs, milk, sugar, and all for a cake, and in a book there's plot, characters, and setting. She said you can add extra, special ingredients, too, to please yourself. Then you let it bake awhile."

"That's all there is to it?"

"Nope. She said the hard part is after it comes out

of the oven. You have to taste it. And if it doesn't taste just right, you may have to throw it out and start all over again. And even if it's pretty good as it is, you still need to add the frosting, the finishing touches. She said that in writing that's called revising."

"Let me guess. You want to be a writer when you grow up."

"That or an archaeologist. Mrs. Madoc had us try writing a mystery of our own. We voted on all the basic stuff, like how old the characters were going to be and what their names were and what crime they had to solve. Then she had each of us write down what we thought would happen in the story. She said to keep asking ourselves 'what if' and we'd never run out of ideas. And she said that even though we were all starting with the same stuff, we'd still end up with lots of different stories by the time we were done."

"And did you?" They'd reached New Portsmouth and Linnea easily found the turn that led to the town library. New Portsmouth was ten times the size of Austin's Crossing, but that still wasn't saying a lot. She'd been surprised to learn from Jen that the community center had a fully equipped gym and a pool. An average of three afternoons a week, Jen went to physical-therapy sessions there.

"Pretty much," Cassie answered. "I was the only one who put in a secret tunnel."

Chuckling, Linnea parked in front of the library, pausing to collect the home-repair books due back that day. They let the dogs out for a quick romp, then tied their leashes to a lamppost.

Inside the library, the librarian greeted both her and Cassie like old friends.

"You remember that book on the Underground Railroad you brought back last time?" she asked Cassie. "I thought of something after you left. I was able to find a newspaper article about it."

She handed the clipping over, then explained further for Linnea's benefit. "There were rumors for years of a tunnel over in Franklin County. It was supposed to run from under the old Wilton Academy building into the basement of a nearby house. When the academy burned down some years back, they hunted for one, but they never found anything. I'm afraid that's the way with most legends. More wishful thinking than fact."

All this talk of history sparked a related thought for Linnea, and when Cassie had gone off to the lower level of the building to browse in the children's section, Linnea consulted the helpful librarian. "Do you have anything here on the history of Austin's Crossing? I'm curious about the house I'm living in."

"There's a bit in the county history, but I can probably tell you as much. You know the houses were built by two brothers?"

"That's what Jen Austin said."

"She would know. One brother had a son, so the family name stayed with that house. The other had just one daughter, and she married a Dennison, so over time that place came to be called the Dennison house. In the next generation, an Austin girl married a Dennison boy, linking the families a second time."

She sketched out a rough genealogy on a yellow lined pad, and talked knowledgeably about second cousins once removed and third cousins twice removed, and lost Linnea entirely by the time she was finished. Linnea got the gist of it, though. She was distantly related to Jen and Marsh Austin, though not to Cassie, who was the child of Marsh's mother's second marriage. There had been, she also gathered, a messy divorce when Marsh was around five years old. His father had left town, enlisted in the military, and been killed in combat in Vietnam a couple of years later.

So she and Marsh were related.

The term *kissing cousin* came to mind, but she forced it back out. By the time she decided to borrow *The History of Jefferson County: 1790–1950* and had selected two mystery novels, she'd also resolved not to dwell any longer on the insidious appeal of her distractingly sexy next-door neighbor.

They'd just have to go back to being friends.

She smiled to herself at the thought.

Friends? They hadn't been friends before and weren't now. Not with the way they grated on each other's nerves. Their relationship was more like an armed truce than a peaceful coexistence.

At least it was never dull.

On the way back to Austin's Crossing, Cassie took up a new topic of conversation, one that made Linnea wish she'd go back to talking about secret tunnels and hidden rooms. "We haven't started that 3-D puzzle yet," she said. "Can we work on it this afternoon?"

" 'Fraid not, Cassie. This afternoon I have to finish painting that woodwork. I want to start wallpapering tomorrow morning."

"I can help."

Inwardly, Linnea groaned. The girl would certainly try, but that morning's experience had proven that when Cassie painted, she got as much on the hardwood floor and on herself as she did on the wide baseboards. Her kind of help would put Linnea's timetable in serious jeopardy. She hated to hurt Cassie's feelings, but she really didn't have any choice.

"I kind of need to work alone this afternoon."

"Why can't I help?"

Linnea sighed softly. "I can finish faster on my own, Cassie. I'm sorry, but that's just the way it is."

"You don't want me around."

Oops. Sulks. Now what?

"Hey, we just spent the morning together. And I'll be over at your house this evening."

"I thought you were different from Anita," Cassie mumbled.

"Anita? Who's Anita?"

"Marsh was going to marry her, but she wanted to live in the city and he wanted to live here. I'm glad he didn't marry her, but I suppose he's got to marry somebody one of these days."

Linnea nearly drove off the road. When her heart rate steadied, she risked a glance at her passenger. Cassie had a hopeful expression on her thin face.

"Don't start what-iffing about me, Cassie. Or matchmaking. I don't know how your brother feels about acquiring a wife, but I'm definitely not in the market for a husband."

That put a damper on conversation until they were back in Austin's Crossing. Once Linnea parked the car, though, Cassie snapped back to her usual agreeable self.

"We have a secret panel at our house. Want to see?"

"If it's a secret, maybe I shouldn't."

"It's okay. It's more of a hidey-hole. Marsh showed it to me when he first came back to Maine."

Came back to Maine? From where? And how long had he been away? Linnea's conscience warred with her curiosity. She shouldn't be questioning Cassie about her brother. On the other hand, when Marsh evaded direct questions and refused to volunteer a single thing about himself . . .

"Where had he been living before that?"

"Boston." Cassie hopped out of the car and released the dogs from the back.

Boston. A city. She wanted very badly to know what he'd done for a living there. And how he'd injured his leg. But pumping a child for information was reprehensible. She was appalled that she'd let the first question slip out.

In a matter-of-fact tone of voice that reminded Linnea of Jen, Cassie volunteered just a bit more. "He'd probably still be living there," she said, "and probably married to old Anita, too, if he hadn't gotten shot."

Shot?

Shock kept Linnea silent as Cassie's chatter revealed that Marsh had only been back in Austin's Crossing a little less than two years. He'd returned after their mother's death. Before that, he hadn't lived there since he left home to start college.

Abruptly, Cassie stopped speaking.

"You okay?" Linnea asked, almost certain Cassie was thinking about losing her mother.

A weak smile answered her. And then, shaking off her sadness, Cassie reverted to her earlier enthusiasm. "Come on. I'll show you where Marsh says he used to hide from alien invaders."

Intrigued by the idea that Marsh might once have had as active an imagination as his half sister, Linnea followed.

They walked up to the front of the house, and with the ease of long familiarity, Cassie reached out toward what appeared to be a solid section of clapboard siding. At her touch, a two-foot square detached itself and slid slowly, quietly, and smoothly down and out. Cassie set it aside to reveal a dark crawl space beneath the Austins' front porch.

"Secret panel," Cassie proclaimed, "and secret tunnel. Or hidey-hole." And then, before Linnea could even think about stopping her, she hoisted herself up and began to wriggle into the depths.

"Cassie, come out of there before you get filthy."

She didn't even want to think about spiders and snakes.

A delighted, almost triumphant giggle answered her. "Now you sound just like a mother," Cassie said.

That comparison left Linnea feeling uneasy for the rest of the day.

SEVEN

She was coming over for supper. Marsh wasn't sure how he felt about that. Not after this morning. How had he ever thought she was too skinny, too flat-chested for his taste? All day long he'd been remembering how she'd felt in his arms, how delicious her lips had tasted, how intoxicated he'd been from the scent of the skin near her ear.

Good thing his ladder was broken beyond repair. If he'd been able to fix it, if he'd had to continue the plan to paint the exterior of her house today, he'd have been hard-pressed to climb back up toward her bedroom window with any equanimity. Keeping his balance would have been a definite problem, even with a brand-new, solid rung ladder.

If he had any sense, he'd be thinking of ways to put some distance between them right now. But he didn't have much sense, and tonight the choice wasn't his. He hadn't even been consulted about asking their neighbor over to eat. Aunt Jen had simply announced Linnea was coming, and when dinner was ready, she ordered him to go fetch her.

The last thing Marsh expected when he approached her back door was to be hit by baking smells. Cautiously, he inhaled again. No mistake. Fresh bread. Blueberry pie. And something with cinnamon in it.

Linnea spotted him through the window. "Oh, good," she said, so brightly that he was sure she felt as uneasy as he did. "You can help carry stuff."

She met him at the door between the mud room and kitchen, redolent of the same scents that filled the room. Cinnamon perfume, he decided, was an erotic, arousing fragrance.

He hoped she was unaware of the full effect she was having on him, but he could tell from her amused smile that she sensed some of his confusion. "I told you I could cook," she reminded him as she waved him inside.

Keep it light, he warned himself. Aloud, he said, "This is baking."

"Close enough. Anyway, preparing food isn't an art. It's a craft learned by trial and error."

"Sure you don't mean trial and terror? Last time Cassie decided to make supper, we had to eat ribs so blackened on the grill that the charcoal fell off them in giant chips."

"Ah—the true test of love. For a friend of mine, I once ate veal so rare it could almost get up and gallop away."

Kathy Lynn Emerson
108

Love?

For a moment he imagined Linnea was talking about another man, a lover, and he was shocked by the intensity of his reaction. Well, hell. He was jealous.

It was okay to be concentrating on getting her into bed. That was purely physical. Jealousy was an emotion, though. He was supposed to be avoiding those.

"Then there's my mother," she continued. "She makes chicken so dry, it takes three glasses of water to choke it down." She gave him a hard look. "Do you realize you scowl rather fiercely every single time I mention Mother?"

"It's nothing. Old news."

"Not if she still annoys you that much after all this time. I mean, you have my sympathy. She annoys the hell out of me. Has since I was Cassie's age and realized she was always going to be too busy to do more than interfere in my life."

"Let it be, Linnea. We need to get going or the ham will be cold."

"I like ham," she said obligingly. "I bake a lot of it myself. Even the most inexperienced cook has a hard time ruining a ham."

"Can't do much harm to mashed potatoes or tossed salad, either."

"And leftover ham is good in glop," she added as she loaded him down with baked goods.

"Glop?"

She nodded. "The most fail-safe recipe in the world. It has many varieties. All you need to do is toss assorted leftovers, any condensed soup, and a handful of noodles into a skillet and turn on the burner."

"That's glop?"

"That's glop."

Well, hell, he thought as he followed her through the gap in the bushes between her yard and his. He really was starting to like this woman entirely too much.

She's Denise's daughter, he reminded himself. That ought to be enough warning for anyone.

But it wasn't.

Not anymore.

He told himself he could go ahead and like her. He'd just have to make sure liking didn't turn into anything more complicated. Staying away from her was no solution. He'd been a fool to consider it, even briefly. No, the best plan was still to seduce her. He'd just have to bide his time, wait for the right moment . . . maybe ask her to bake again, just for him.

The image of Linnea Bryan standing in her kitchen wearing nothing but aquamarine panties and an old-fashioned, frilly apron, had an embarrassingly obvious effect on him.

His ardor cooled quickly, though, when Jen caught sight of Linnea's pie. "Why that looks as good as the ones Cassandra used to make," she remarked.

The image of his *mother* in Linnea's kitchen expelled the erotic fantasy from Marsh's mind. Picturing her also brought back, with painful intensity, the memory of one of the last times he'd talked to her.

She'd accused him of leaving her.

There was irony for you. She'd left him first. She'd just been trying to lay a guilt trip on him, to make sure he'd take care of Cassie after she was gone. He knew that now. At the time he'd just been angry. He'd let it show, too, his subconscious way of punishing her for remarrying when he was a confused boy of fourteen, and leaving him behind to go off with her new husband.

While he'd stayed in Austin's Crossing with his paternal grandparents, she'd traveled to New York and London and Paris with Lowell Graham, Cassie's father. Bright city lights had called to her, just as they'd lured Denise away.

Just as they'd eventually enticed Marsh himself.

"Marsh?" Aunt Jen's voice penetrated his gloomy recollections, bringing him back to the present with a start. Back to Linnea. And to Cassie.

He had come back home for Cassie's sake after their mother's death, but it was the best move he'd ever made for himself too. The worst had been leaving Austin's Crossing in the first place.

The meal passed uneventfully enough, but afterward, over cups of coffee and slices of Linnea's pie, while Cassie was off looking for a book she wanted to show Linnea, Jen remarked upon the rapport between Cassie and Linnea.

"I worry that Cassie may be getting a bit too attached to me," Linnea said.

"Oh, surely not," Aunt Jen said.

"How so?" Marsh asked, careful to keep his voice neutral. He supposed he shouldn't be surprised that

Linnea was troubled by the same thing that had bothered him. She was always throwing him curves.

"Girls her age are very impressionable," Linnea said. "I don't think she really believes I mean to leave when the house is finished. In fact . . ." She glanced quickly at Marsh, then away. "I think she's starting to see herself as a matchmaker."

"Well, hell."

"Exactly."

"Perhaps you're making too much of this," Aunt Jen suggested. "Cassie has a great ability to bounce back from little disappointments. She told me you wouldn't let her paint anymore because she was clumsy."

"I never said she was clumsy!"

"You didn't have to. She has eyes. My point is that you needn't worry too much. Let her down easy, as you have so far, and she'll cope. And if all else fails, school will be starting soon. She'll become occupied with other things."

"She could be occupied with other things now," Linnea said, giving Marsh another, more direct look. "It's you she'd really like to be spending time with, you know. Maybe you ought to consider helping me less and working jigsaw puzzles with her more."

Marsh fought down a flare of resentment. He didn't like being lectured to. "I don't think so," he said in a sharper tone than he'd intended.

The sound of Cassie's returning footsteps put an end to the discussion, but Marsh couldn't easily dismiss it from his mind. He knew he ought to be spend-

ing more time with Cassie. And Linnea would do well
to spend less time with her. Ironic, that. If he continued with his plans for Linnea, Cassie might end up
resenting both of them for ignoring her.

Or be convinced there was a wedding in the future.

Both troubling thoughts.

Linnea's next comment bothered him almost as
much. While he'd been brooding she and Jen had
begun talking about Old Man Dennison.

"It just seems odd to me," Linnea was saying,
"that my grandfather passed over my mother to leave
the house to me. There has to be some logical explanation. What did she do to get herself disowned?"

"You should ask your mother that," Jen advised.
Marsh thought his aunt looked uncomfortable. How
much *did* Jen know? he wondered.

"She won't talk about Austin's Crossing." Linnea
shot a fulminating look in Marsh's direction. "She's as
bad as some other people I know about answering
direct questions."

"Perhaps the explanation is very simple, then," Jen
suggested. "Your grandfather knew your mother never
intended to come back. He hoped you would."

"I asked Emma if she remembered my grandfather."

Marsh tensed. "And?"

Linnea's shrug and grimace relieved his mind even
before she repeated the old woman's words. "She said
he was eccentric and that my mother just up and disappeared one day."

"That's about right," Jen said.

"Someone must remember more about him than that."

And if she found someone who did, Marsh thought, that someone might also tell her exactly why her mother "just up and disappeared one day." The only way he could think of to keep her from stumbling over information she shouldn't have was to offer to help her track down sources himself.

"There's one person who might talk to you about your grandfather," he said slowly. "Dennison did always keep to himself. Not a real friendly sort. But he was only a little older than Emma's brother Bob. If there's anyone around who'd still remember what Howard Dennison was like when he was a young man, it would be Bob Farley."

Without quite knowing how, Marsh ended up promising to take Linnea over to Farley's place the next day. He could only hope he hadn't just made a huge mistake.

One part of Linnea's brain understood that she was asleep. In her dream, though, a thump woke her. She saw herself sit up in bed and was aware she was in a hotel room in a strange city.

At first she thought a pigeon must have flown into the window glass. She peered toward the source of the sound, more puzzled than panic-stricken, until starlight's pale gleam revealed a clinging hand. When a second set of fingers joined the first, her breath caught in her throat.

Impossible as it seemed, someone was out there.

The hands shifted. One got a better grip while the other pushed at the bottom of the window, trying to lift it higher.

With the illogic of a dreamer, Linnea didn't try to scream or call for help. Instead she swung her legs over the side of the bed and floated toward the window. She knew she had to rescue him, or spend the rest of her life feeling responsible for his death.

"Thanks," a muffled voice said as she pushed the window up. She looked down and saw his dark shape dangling below her. And then he moved, pulling himself slowly upward and into the room.

She started to reach for a light switch, but steely fingers closed around her ankle and pulled, jerking her off balance. An instant later she was flat on her back.

As the dream threatened to turn into a nightmare, Linnea finally tried to scream. She managed only a whimper. The cat burglar—for she knew he was one—surged up along her side and clamped one gloved hand over her mouth.

Instinctively, she fought him. She was in good shape, but he was bigger, stronger, and desperate besides. He rolled her beneath him, holding her down with his weight and trapping her arms between their chests. The lower part of his torso was perfectly aligned with hers, and when he landed squarely in the cradle of her thighs, she was vibrantly aware of his masculinity.

A new kind of panic made her fight harder. "I

saved your life," she protested the moment he removed his hand. "How can you do this to me?"

She managed to work one arm free and clawed at his eyes. Her fingers encountered the rough wool of a ski mask just before he caught her wrist and immobilized her again, jerking her hand over her head and pinning it to the floor.

The change in position brought his upper body into contact with her breasts. Linnea arched upward in another futile attempt to dislodge him. He countered by pressing her more deeply into the carpet. His face was only inches above her own and she could feel his warm breath on her cheek. She went perfectly still.

As soon as she stopped struggling, he loosened his grip. Then, very slowly, as if he didn't quite trust her not to knee him in the groin, he allowed her to sit up. She tugged her cotton nightgown back down over her bare legs, glad that the garment was floor-length. During the struggle it had hiked up to well above her knees.

They sat on the floor, a foot of space between them. The position gave a strange intimacy to a situation that already reeked of surrealism. Although the room was in semidarkness and he was dressed all in black, she could see enough of him to confirm what she'd felt when she'd been crushed beneath him—he had a wonderfully muscular physique, the hard and lean workingman's kind rather than the bulging, overdeveloped look of the self-involved bodybuilder.

"Like what you see?" he asked in Marsh Austin's most irritated voice.

The instant Linnea recognized it, she came awake for real.

"Well, hell," she muttered, stealing one of Marsh's own expressions.

Now what, exactly, did that flight of fancy mean?

That she trusted him, even with all her questions unanswered? Maybe. That she was attracted to him? She readily admitted that. That she was curious about his past? Obviously, especially after the juicy bits Cassie had let slip earlier. She wanted to know exactly how he'd gotten injured, too, but she was pretty certain it hadn't been climbing into hotel rooms via the window.

Linnea groaned. Analyze. Understand. That was the best way to deal with a bad dream. Or she could chalk it up to too many slices of pie with ice cream on top and try to forget the shockingly sensual details.

She ended up trying both methods . . . and didn't get another wink of sleep all night.

Marsh paused in between the pocket doors and watched in amusement as Linnea struggled with a long strip of flowered and flocked wallpaper. She used a small stepladder to reach the top of the wall, then slowly descended, easing the paper into position as she went. She was stooping to smooth the lower section with her brush before she realized she'd cut the piece too short. At least an inch of bare plaster wall showed at the bottom.

A colorful curse was followed by a yelp of surprise

as the upper part of the wallpaper detached itself and landed on her head.

"I'm going to start charging for rescuing you," Marsh muttered as he stepped into the room. A couple of steps brought him close enough to seize the end of the enveloping curl of paper.

Her gasp brought him up short.

He'd startled her, he knew, but that had sounded more like fear. He took a step back and let her fight her way free on her own. Once she emerged, he studied her flushed face, the stiff set of her shoulders. Something had her riled up, but he didn't think he'd done anything new.

Unless he was supposed to have walked her home last night, followed her up to the attic, and made love to her. Had she wanted him to? That hadn't been the impression he'd gotten after they'd agreed he'd introduce her to Bob Farley. She'd excused herself, saying it had been a long day, and had all but bolted out of his house and into hers.

"What's got into you this afternoon?" he demanded when she kept staring at him, not speaking, barely breathing. It was as if she was waiting for him to attack her or something.

"Bad dream last night," she answered.

"Well, don't take it out on me."

"Why not? You were in it."

"Yeah?" That sounded promising. She'd been in his dreams a few times lately too. Including last night. "Doing what?"

"Keeping me awake." The sharply spoken words

were tempered by a blush. And damned if she wasn't doing one of those shy, beneath-the-lashes glances in his direction. When she added, "Do me a favor, will you?" his imagination went into overdrive.

"If I can."

"Satisfy my curiosity."

He opened his arms wide and stepped toward her. "Ah, Linnea, I thought you'd never ask." He wasn't really surprised when she backed away, her fulminating glare firmly back in place. Grinning, he drawled, "It was worth a shot."

"I want information, Marsh. Honesty."

Stung by the implication he hadn't been honest with her, and knowing the accusation was more true than he liked to admit, he gave her a curt nod, indicating she should continue. Since it looked like it was going to be a long discussion, he eased down into one of the sheet-covered chairs. He didn't think he'd ever seen such a serious expression on her face.

"Just tell me straight out," she said, "if you were a good guy or a bad guy before you got injured on the job. Or an innocent bystander," she added as an after-thought, clearly certain the latter was an unlikely possibility. In fact, she sounded like she thought he might have been a crook.

"I was a cop."

"How did you get shot?"

"On duty." In spite of his irritation at her persistent nosiness, he supposed there was no reason not to tell her. It did seem mighty important to her all of a sudden. "I took one bullet in the arm, another in the hip. I am now officially disabled, at least in the sense that I can no longer do the job I was trained for."

"No wonder you don't like cities."

Once again she'd managed to surprise him with her reaction. He searched for the right response and finally went with, "It's no place to bring a kid up in, that's for sure."

"So you moved back here for Cassie's sake?"

"Not entirely."

"You stayed away a long time."

"I was stupid."

He'd gone looking for adventure. He'd been sick of living in the back of beyond, and after college he'd thought he'd find what he wanted in Boston. He hadn't wised up until after he'd nearly lost his life. By then he'd been involved with a woman, a city woman. When his mother died and he ended up with custody of Cassie, Marsh had expected Anita to love him enough to give up the bright lights and move back to Maine with him. Fat chance. She'd countered with the proposal he work for her father in the security business. Cassie, she'd said, could go to a private school.

"You don't trust me, do you?" Linnea asked.

He shrugged. There was no reason to tell her all the details. It wasn't as if she was going to be a permanent part of his life.

"I came back because my roots are here. I belong. You belong back in the big city. The best we can have together is a brief fling. Is that honest enough for you, Linnea?"

She sucked in a breath and turned away for a moment. That was all it took, though, for her to regain her composure. "Well, I'll say one thing. That you were a cop accounts for your suspicious nature. And for your reluctance to talk about yourself unless someone practically cross-examines you."

Grudgingly, he conceded she had a point.

"Only fair, I guess," she went on. "I haven't told you that much about my life. But then, you haven't asked."

At her politely sarcastic words, he felt a belated prickle of guilt. "Since you want honest, I guess I'd better make a confession. I had you investigated before you arrived. I've still got friends in law enforcement. They checked you out. Answered most of the questions I had about you." And then some.

She seemed taken aback, then she smiled and leaned back against a section of newly papered wall, crossing her arms over her chest. "Find out anything interesting?"

He couldn't resist. "You bought aquamarine underwear at a boutique two weeks before you came here." Her blush made him grin. "Got to admit I keep wondering if you're wearing it."

Clearing her throat, Linnea looked everywhere but at him. "Sorry to disappoint you, Marsh, but that purchase was a gift for a friend's wedding shower. I prefer plain white cotton."

"I don't believe it."

"No? Want to take a look in my dresser drawers?"

"How about I go direct to another sort of drawers?"

She was searching for a comeback when they heard the kitchen door slam and the clatter of footsteps headed their way. "History repeats itself," Linnea muttered.

"God, I hope not." She gave him an odd look, but he could hardly explain that he'd been thinking of his father and her mother.

"Hey, you guys," Cassie greeted them as she charged into the room with Foolish at her heels. "Want to help me hunt for an Underground Railroad station?"

"Can't right now," Linnea told her. "Your brother and I are going over to Mr. Farley's so I can ask him about my grandfather."

"I know his grandson," Cassie said. "Chaz used to help out with the dogs. After Aunt Jen had her accident and before my mother died. Then he started college and Marsh came home. Can I go with you?"

"I don't think so, short stuff." Marsh caught Linnea's eye and shook his head, hoping she'd back him up.

It was possible Linnea would learn more that afternoon than he intended. If so, the least he could do was make sure Cassie didn't find out too. He had a responsibility to protect his young sister from hurtful gossip. He knew all too well how hard that could be on a kid.

It surprised him to see a sulky expression flit across Cassie's face. Then she resorted to the big-sad-eyes trick, appealing first to him and then to Linnea.

"I said no, Cassie." His voice was sharper than

he'd intended. Trying to moderate it, he added, "This is grown-up business."

"I'm not going to contradict your brother, Cassie," Linnea said in milder tones.

"Then can I stay here and search Linnea's cellar? You said we could look down there, Linnea. You promised."

"Yes, I did. But not today and not on your own. It's too dangerous. I haven't had a chance to explore the cellar myself, but I do remember seeing several stacks of old furniture and boxes that looked like they could collapse if you breathed on them the wrong way. I think we've had enough of things toppling over for one week. I don't want anyone getting hurt."

The sulks returned, the pouting increased, and Marsh could tell Linnea felt bad about saying no, but she stuck to her guns.

"I'm sorry, Cassie. You'll have to wait until I'm with you. Or until I've had time to clean the place up a bit."

"When?"

"I don't know. Tomorrow?"

Unappeased, Cassie glared at them both. "Can I start work on the puzzle?" she asked Linnea.

"Sure. It's on the card table in the attic."

Well, hell, Marsh thought. That meant Cassie might still be in Linnea's bedroom when they got back from Bob's.

"What about the puzzle you and I were going to start?" he suggested. "That turn-of-the-century train traveling through a Colorado blizzard?"

"The one I got you last Christmas?" Cassie said, turning to him. "The one we were going to work on as soon as school got out?"

Stung by his sister's unexpected sarcasm, Marsh frowned. "Yeah. That one."

He had let her down, but that was no excuse for her disrespectful tone. He was debating whether to say something now or wait till later when Cassie looked back at Linnea.

"I don't think I want to start any jigsaw puzzles. I'll just get stuck finishing them all by myself." With an overly dramatic toss of her head, which set her ponytail bouncing, she ordered, "Come, Foolish!" and flounced out.

"Oh, dear," Linnea murmured. By the expression on her face, she was torn between amusement and concern. "Maybe we should let her come with us, Marsh."

"She can't have her own way all the time." He tried not to let Linnea see how much Cassie's rebellious manner bothered him. It wasn't like her to sass him. And he did feel guilty. He'd been neglecting her.

A week or two ago he'd have tried to place the blame for any deterioration in Cassie's behavior on Linnea. Now, although he wasn't sure why his kid sister was acting up, he was fairly certain it wasn't Linnea's fault.

"Do you suppose it has to do with the fact that school starts soon?" Linnea asked. "She's only got a little more than two weeks of freedom left before she has to go back."

"Maybe. I don't imagine she likes change much."

"Does she like school?"

"She always used to." He frowned. "This year, though, she doesn't seem particularly eager to see her friends again."

"I haven't seen her with a single child her own age since I've been here."

"Meaning?"

As if she'd heard the challenging note in that single word, Linnea hesitated. "I don't know what I mean." She plastered a bright, phony smile on her face and didn't quite meet his eyes. "It isn't any of my business anyway. Let me just change clothes and we can go visit Mr. Farley."

Marsh turned to watch her climb the stairs. Of its own volition, his gaze fixed on her bottom. He looked quickly away, but it was already too late. He spent the next ten minutes in torment, imagining her stripping off her tight jeans to reveal what lay beneath.

He'd always had a weakness for white cotton.

EIGHT

Bargain Bob's Preowned Treasures was a disreputable-looking old shack on the main road. The building was at least as run-down as Linnea's house had been, but like the old Dennison place, Bargain Bob's had its own brand of charm. Constructed from barn boards and extended by a canvas awning off to one side, it appeared to be crammed full of anything and everything.

Bargain Bob himself was Austin's Crossing's village character. Though white-haired, stooped, and nearing, Marsh informed Linnea, his eighty-fifth birthday, he still looked pretty spry to her.

"You must be the Dennison girl," he said after nodding a greeting to Marsh.

"Bryan," Linnea corrected him, "but my mother was Denise Dennison."

"Same difference." Bob fished in his shirt pocket for his pouch of pipe tobacco. "I'm in perfect health," he said when he caught Linnea wrinkling her nose in distaste. He continued to fill the bowl with aromatic tobacco. "If smoking a pipe ain't killed me yet, 'tisn't likely to."

Linnea wasn't about to argue with him, no matter what her personal feelings on the subject. "I've come to you to ask about my grandfather," she said.

Bob nodded slowly. "I knew him. Also know why Denise run off."

Linnea was aware that Marsh had gone very still beside her, but she kept her attention on Bob. "She and her father didn't get along."

"She couldn't stand the old coot. Soon as she had enough money saved to skedaddle, she skedid." Chortling at his own humor, Bob winked at Marsh, who stared stolidly back.

"Did they quarrel?"

"All the time," Bob said.

Linnea thought that if her mother and grandfather clashed the way she and Denise did, it was no wonder her mother had left.

"She couldn'ta been mor'n eighteen. Went up to Portland or somewheres first. Left on the back of a motorcycle with some wild boy she met at the diner over in New Portsmouth."

He referred to the town as if it were hundreds of miles away instead of just down the road, making Linnea wonder how far Bob himself had ever been from home.

"She marry that biker, girl?"

For just a moment Linnea wondered if she had. Then she shrugged. "I don't know."

"Thought maybe he might'a been your daddy."

She smiled at that. "If he was, both he and the motorcycle were long gone before I was old enough to take an interest."

"You never knew your father?" Marsh asked. He sounded shocked.

Linnea wondered why he should be, but this was not the time to ask. She concentrated on Bob instead.

"I know as much as I need to about my mother," she told him, "but I'm very interested in finding out more about my grandfather."

Bob tamped the tobacco into his briar pipe, performing the whole ritual of lighting and sucking and tamping some more before he was ready to tell Linnea what she wanted to know. "Great one for crazy ideas, Howard Dennison was. Craziest thing he ever did was build that bomb shelter."

Smoke rings rose into an already overcast summer sky. Bob watched them contemplatively, aware he had a captive audience. Linnea's eyes narrowed, considering the old man. He was probably trying to decide how much to tell her. Or how much he could get away with inventing. She'd learned a few things about rural humor since her arrival in Maine.

"Must have been forty years ago," Bob finally went on. "Maybe more." He paused to let that sink in.

"And?" Marsh prompted him. He seemed more at ease now.

"Back then," Bob continued, "folks all over this

great land of ours was expecting them Russians to drop the bomb. There was lots of articles in all the magazines about what would happen to you depending on how far you was from the place the bomb actually hit. Fallout and all. And there was pieces on bomb shelters. How to build one. What to store inside."

"Are you saying my grandfather went out and built a bomb shelter?"

"That's the story." Bob sucked on his pipe with a noise that set Linnea's teeth on edge and took his time about expanding on his answer. "Kept talking about protecting what was his. And there was all these deliveries for a while. Cinder blocks. Cement. That sort of thing. But no one ever knew for sure what he did with them."

Skepticism growing, Linnea waited for a punch line. She glanced at Marsh, but he only shrugged, which lent credibility to her theory that Bob was pulling her leg. Surely Marsh's family would have known if her grandfather had built something so . . . big. At the least they'd have heard the noise of construction.

Bob seemed content to puff away on the pipe, letting her think about what he'd said. It was Marsh who finally broke the silence. "So, Bob. You never saw the finished bomb shelter?"

"Nope. Never did. Don't even know for sure where he planned to put it. Underground, I expect. Do know he was a secretive cuss. And not very neighborly. Good thing there never was no atom bomb come down here in Austin's Crossing. He'd have left the rest of us to fry."

"You mean he wouldn't have let his friends in if there was an attack?" Linnea asked.

"Would you?"

"Well, of course."

"You think about it, missy." Bob started to chuckle. Then he started to choke. Marsh pounded him on the back, and by the time Bob recovered, tears were streaming down his deeply lined and wrinkled smoker's face.

"Letting anyone else in would have defeated the purpose," Marsh said to her.

"I still don't get it."

"Here's the way it was, missy," Bob said. "Fella builds himself a place to keep safe in during a nuclear attack. Bombs start dropping. He scampers inside and closes the door. He's got what's important to him in there with him. Then the neighbors come along and pound on the door."

Marsh's father? His grandparents? Linnea nodded for Bob to go on.

"He opens up, radiation comes in with them. No, sir. Howard Dennison mighta been crazy as a loon, but he weren't no fool. The way I remember him, he'd've yelled 'You go-o-o-o to the dev-i-il!' and kept the entrance tight closed."

"But the people outside would have died!" What kind of person had her grandfather been? The story upset Linnea a great deal. She was no longer sure she wanted to find out more about her family.

Bob's pipe had gone out again and he was fussing with it. "If it'd been me on the outside, about to die,

I'd have been mad enough to take that selfish old coot with me."

"How?" Marsh asked.

Linnea shot him an appalled look. Wasn't what she was imagining bad enough already?

"There'd have been an air duct somewhere," Bob said. "I'd a found it and crammed it full of leaves or some such and taken him to the devil with me."

A shudder racked Linnea, and she decided she was more than ready to put an end to this conversation. "I can't think of anything worse than being trapped underground without air."

" 'Cept bein' outside with the radiation. Don't forget that, missy." Bargain Bob was still chortling and puffing on his pipe when they got into Marsh's truck to drive the mile and a half back to Austin's Crossing.

"Please tell me," Linnea said, "that that whole story is as preposterous as Cassie's chances of finding an entrance to an Underground Railroad station. I feel like I should be apologizing to you for my grandfather being so unneighborly."

"No need." He slanted a look in her direction, startling her with the decidedly amorous gleam in his eyes. "But if it really bothers you, I'm sure you can think of some way to make it up to me."

Several hours later Marsh and Linnea had cleared the cellar of obvious dangers, finished hanging the wallpaper in the living room, and shared a meal of

Linnea's famous glop. Rain sheeted down outside as she washed and he dried the dishes.

"I do owe you one apology," she said as she handed him a freshly scrubbed cooking pot.

"For what?"

"Insisting you tell me about your injury. It wasn't any of my business."

"Why was it so important that you know?"

He was expecting an admission of personal interest. They'd been building toward intimacy all day. Instead he got, in detail, an account of the dream she'd had the previous night. Those lingering images, she insisted, had been to blame for her snoopiness.

"Though I was somehow sure," she added, "even when I was having the dream, that the cat burglar was a good guy. Probably a private detective on some sort of secret mission."

The dishes were finished. She reached out to take the damp towel from him, but he wouldn't release it. Their hands touched. Marsh could almost see the sparks. He could most definitely feel them.

"I wish I'd stayed asleep long enough to find out how that dream was going to end," she whispered.

He shook his head. "No, what you really wanted to know was how those kisses we shared yesterday morning were going to end."

He leaned toward her until he could brush her lips with his. She responded sweetly, encouraging him to deepen the kiss.

"Linnea, I want to take you to bed."

He made no promises, but he was pretty sure she

knew he was no dream lover. She wouldn't go imagining things about him. Like him, she wasn't interested in more than what they could share in the here and now.

She delayed only long enough to lock the door, then led him up to her bedroom under the eaves.

Summer rain drummed down on the roof above the bed. Cooling night air, carrying just a little of the moisture, gusted toward them through the half-open windows.

Perfect, Linnea thought.

Just the right atmosphere.

Just the right man.

Tenderly, as if he were unwrapping a priceless statue, he divested her of her clothing, pausing to smile when he encountered the promised white cotton. "Always have been partial to practical women," he murmured.

She might have wished she had on the aquamarine silk she'd bought for her friend, if the heat in Marsh's eyes hadn't reassured her. He was quite happy with what he'd found. He seemed even more pleased when he removed that last barrier and stroked bare skin.

If there was a tiny part of Linnea's heart that wished he would make a declaration of undying devotion to her, she ruthlessly suppressed it. She'd wanted to know what it would be like to make love with Marsh Austin. She was about to find out. She was not going to blow it by babbling on about her feelings for him.

This was what she wanted. It was what she'd wanted probably since the first moment she'd laid eyes on him.

It just wasn't *all* she wanted.

"Hey," she protested as he stepped back and took a very long, very hard look at all he'd uncovered. "I don't want to be the only one here who's naked."

"Don't worry. You won't be."

Any lingering self-consciousness fled before his admiring gaze. And then she forgot entirely about how she might look to him. Truthfully, she could barely think at all as his body was revealed to her. The sight of all that male flesh literally took her breath away.

There wasn't an ounce of excess fat anywhere on his lean, muscular frame. Her gaze lingered on a faint scar on his arm, then shifted to his chest, where a soft mat of dark, curly hair arrowed downward. Mesmerized, she stared at his hands as he removed his jeans and his briefs in one economical movement.

Swallowing hard, she decided nothing less than a nuclear blast could force her to look away now. He was apparently unconcerned by her intense scrutiny, but definitely not unaffected. "Oh, my," she murmured as she got a good look at the delights in store for her.

Grinning, he bent to gather up his discarded clothing. Linnea found herself staring at the top of his head, at the thick, dark hair that had been one of the first things she'd ever noticed about him.

She was about to reach out and undo the leather thong that held his queue, when he distracted her yet again by turning to put the clothes on a nearby chair. Her mouth went dry, then began to water as he presented her with a tantalizing view of a firm, masculine backside.

Only belatedly did Linnea realize that his movement also revealed to her gaze the extensive damage to his leg. Her attention shifted to his hip and the outside of his thigh. Even after two years the legacy of what bullets and surgery had done was still quite visible. It was a wonder he had only a slight limp.

"Ugly, I'm afraid." He caught her chin and lifted her face for a kiss, forcing her to stop staring at his scars. "You, on the other hand, are perfect."

"Hardly." She didn't want to be, not when he'd suffered such grievous wounds.

"I don't see any blemishes." Lying on the bed beside her, he stretched her out so he could look her up and down. Then he began to kiss her, starting at her toes, touching her with his lips everywhere his gaze had been.

Erotic excitement hummed from each point his mouth caressed, but even as she reached for him and kissed him back, Linnea was wishing for some way to convince him that his scars didn't seem ugly to her. They were just . . . part of the man she loved.

The realization that she'd gone and fallen in love

with Marsh Austin jolted her, but she retained enough sense not to say the words aloud.

As if he sensed some sudden change in her, he paused, lifting his head from her breast to look into her eyes. "Linnea?"

Knowing she had to say something, that he would stop doing all those wonderful things to her body if she hesitated, she said the first thing that came to mind. "I'm not perfect."

"You are from where I'm lying."

"Nope."

She did have scars. Not much compared with his, and they'd come from dog bites. That wouldn't be the best thing to bring up. She didn't want to remind him of how fearful she'd been the first time she'd met his prized huskies.

"I do have a . . . flaw."

She lowered her voice on the last word, hoping that restoring the familiar banter between them would ease her own anxiety. Her unexpected discovery that she was in love with him had thrown her for a loop. She still wasn't thinking clearly.

"What flaw?" He was smiling, amused and turned on at the same time. "A mole? A dimple? No, let me guess. You've got a bunion."

Laughing with him, she put one hand on each side of his face and kissed him hard. "You'll never guess," she said.

"Confess, then."

She giggled. "Teeth."

"Teeth?"

"Yup."

"No way. Smile for me." She did, and he kissed each side of her mouth before he peered inside. "Not crooked that I can see. No fangs."

Kisses landed on his nose, her eyebrow.

"Look closer," she said. "How many other people have you known who have four front teeth all the same size?"

She expected more laughter. Instead, Marsh froze, staring in disbelief at the mouth he'd so recently kissed.

"My dentist thinks they're a hoot," she said weakly. A feeling of impending disaster was growing deep inside her. "He also assured me it's extremely rare to find someone with four front teeth like mine, instead of the usual two."

Marsh scrambled to get off the bed, away from her. The moment he was on his feet, he grabbed for his clothes, covering himself.

"How many other people have I known with those teeth?" he repeated. "Try three. Aunt Jen. My father. And my grandfather. Those are Austin teeth, Linnea."

Struggling to sit up, disconcerted enough to flip the brocade bedspread over her own nakedness, Linnea watched in confusion as he backed toward the stairs. "What on earth are you talking about?"

"Austin teeth."

"Meaning?"

"Meaning I didn't happen to inherit them from my father, but apparently he did pass them on to his daughter."

That took a minute to work out. Then she stared at him, incredulous. "Our parents had an affair? My mother and your father? And you think you and I are brother and sister?"

With only a nod for an answer, he all but ran from the room. She went after him. Wrapped in brocaded silk, she was downstairs within a minute of his dramatic departure from her bed.

The rain that had seemed so romantic earlier now made the whole world bleak. He was waiting for her in the gloomy living room. This time, he'd removed the drop cloths from her two easy chairs before he sat in one.

"Explain," she demanded.

"It never even occurred to me until today. For just an instant back at Bargain Bob's, when he was asking about your father, I let myself contemplate the worst-case scenario, that your father was also mine." His voice sounded lifeless.

"Obviously you talked yourself out of it." Linnea hated hearing her own sarcasm, but she couldn't help her tone. If he'd only told her sooner, this whole traumatic scene might have been avoided.

"I figured you were too young. Denise left town nearly two years before you were born. Though my father left soon after she did, I didn't think he ever saw her again, but I was never certain. I was much too young myself at the time to be aware of anything except the fact that my father wasn't living with us anymore. The loss of my favorite baby-sitter was minor in comparison to that. It was only years later that I connected the two events."

He closed his eyes, as if to ward off pain. Linnea knew how he felt. They were in the middle of a nightmare and she wanted very badly to wake up.

"And now," he went on, "I see their affair accounts for your obvious Austin heritage."

"Keep talking, Marsh. I want to know everything you do."

She knew she now sounded cold and unfeeling, but he'd hurt her. He'd been keeping secrets from her all along. Marsh Austin, the man she'd thought epitomized honesty. The man with whom she'd foolishly gone and fallen in love.

Marsh told the whole story of the tawdry affair between his father and her mother, and when he finished he realized Linnea wasn't nearly as upset as she should be. It seemed impossible to him, but with each added detail, she got calmer.

"I don't buy it," she said when he sent a questioning look her way.

"What part don't you buy? The affair happened. It broke up my parents' marriage. Drove my father away."

"But not to my mother's waiting arms."

"Oh, no? The evidence says otherwise." He stared hard at her mouth.

"My biological and legal father is named Larry Bryan and he's alive and well, if somewhat hard to communicate with. Mother married him six months after she left Austin's Crossing and she gave birth to me a full year and a half later. I don't know if he was the boy on the motorcycle. I'll have to ask. They divorced when I was two."

"Pardon my skepticism, but Denise could have been seeing my father on the side. How else do you explain the Austin teeth?"

"Not into family history, are you?"

"Not particularly. I didn't have much appreciation of family before I came home again."

"For a man who breeds animals, you are astonishingly thick. I got my Austin blood generations ago. Twice over. Remember those two brothers who built the houses?"

"How can you be sure that's all it is? My father—"

She waved away his objections. "If you'd ever heard my mother list my faults, you wouldn't have a doubt in the world that I'm a Bryan. Everything she dislikes, she says I inherited from that side of the family."

Marsh stared at her intently, not just at her mouth this time, but into her eyes, as if he could find the real truth there. One thing was immediately clear. She believed what she was saying. Maybe she was even right. He hoped so. "Comes down to trusting what Denise told you," he muttered.

A glare answered that comment. "Yes," she said in an icy tone. She hadn't been all that upset before, but it was building now. Her eyes flashed fire even as her voice stayed cold as hoarfrost. "I can confirm it with my father, with a blood test, with any method you like, though I don't suppose there's much point in that now. You hardly look like a man who wants to sleep with me at the moment."

"Linnea—"

"Oh, please. Don't apologize. I understand a great deal about our relationship now, you see. You've had me confused with my mother all along."

"You're nothing like your mother." And he'd been incapable, at five, of feeling what he felt now, as a man, for Linnea.

"How nice of you to notice. Too bad you didn't figure that out weeks ago. All that 'city girl' stuff was directed at her, wasn't it? I've just been a stand-in for your anger at her."

He'd stopped confusing the two women some time back, but he didn't know how to convince Linnea of that. Under any other circumstances he'd have tried taking her in his arms, but he didn't guess she'd be very receptive to that approach right now.

An uncomfortable silence settled between them. Marsh was achingly aware that they'd almost made love . . . and that he'd probably had no real reason to stop.

"You'd better go," she finally said.

He went.

NINE

On Labor Day weekend the people of Austin's Crossing turned out to paint the outside of Linnea's house and tear down her wreck of a barn. It should have been one of the happiest times of her life. At last she felt she was truly part of this small community, as though she'd been accepted by her neighbors.

The entire event was as old-fashioned and "country" as you could get, and she loved every minute of it. Except that Marsh wasn't there. He had to work at the store.

"Someone had to," Jen said, giving her a comforting pat on the arm. "Market won't run itself."

Forcing a smile, Linnea went back into the house to make more sandwiches. She'd be surprised if the market had a single customer that day. They were all here, being neighborly.

And Marsh was behind it, she'd bet her Mustang on it.

Just because the two of them had barely spoken for more than two weeks didn't mean he wasn't thinking about her, or feeling he'd let her down by not finishing the painting himself. She'd certainly wasted inordinate amounts of time reliving her own memories.

Before he'd even been out her door that night, she had wanted to call him back. She'd wished more than anything that she could simply erase time and return to the moment before she'd stupidly mentioned her teeth.

Her teeth! How absurd. How heartbreaking.

And now there was this barrier between them. Not that they were related. That was nonsense. The barrier came from all the emotional baggage Marsh had apparently been carrying around ever since his father had deserted him and his mother.

Linnea had eventually phoned her own mother, of course. She'd hung up vindicated on one score . . . and shocked down to her toes on another. Marsh's father wasn't her father. Denise hadn't seen him for more than a year before Linnea's birth. However, she had contacted him once after she left Maine.

She'd extorted enough money from Marsh's father to start the company that had later made her a fortune. It wouldn't have existed at all if it hadn't been for Austin money.

Linnea was resolved to find some way to make up that loss to the Austin family. Unfortunately, Marsh wouldn't even talk about it. When she'd told him, he'd just shrugged and said, "Sounds like Denise."

A soft, female voice from behind her jerked Linnea

back to the present. "You've done a good job with this place."

Linnea smiled over her shoulder at Marsh's part-time assistant, a small, white-haired lady with an energetic look about her. "Hello, Emma. Thank you."

Structural repairs had been made early on. Once today's work was done, only the interior finishing touches would be left. Linnea hadn't even started the three bedrooms on the second floor, but she had plenty of time. Her four months wouldn't be up until mid-November.

"Smells better too," Emma added with a grin.

"Oh, you mean my grandfather's cats?" Linnea had heard that he'd had a veritable horde of them. "What happened to them when he died, anyway?"

As soon as the question was out, she wished she hadn't asked. If they'd been put to sleep, she didn't want to know.

Emma's answer was reassuring. "We found good homes for all of them. My husband and I took several of them ourselves."

"Thank you."

"Helped keep the mice down at the store."

Linnea knew that Marsh had bought the market from Emma soon after his return to Austin's Crossing. Since Emma and her husband had owned and operated the place until his death, the deal had also given her life interest in the living quarters upstairs.

"Of course," Emma went on, "some people around here are more partial to dogs."

Foolish, Tatupu, and Fluffernutter, an all-white,

blue-eyed lead dog, were outside. Their presence no longer made Linnea nervous. She'd been more edgy about spending the day with so many people she'd never met before.

"The Austins are sure the dog lovers in this town," Emma persisted.

With a sudden rush of warmth, Linnea realized what Emma's words meant. She'd been accepted. Emma was trying to initiate conversation . . . no, gossip. For a moment she let herself savor the sense of belonging. Unexpectedly, she even began to wish she could stay here longer than the four months she'd planned on.

"The Siberian huskies are beautiful animals," she said aloud.

"And expensive. The Austins are the only ones in these parts who could afford to keep so many."

"I didn't think Marsh was particularly wealthy," Linnea blurted out, surprised into speaking before she thought through what she said.

"Family ran the old general store, back at the turn of the century," Emma said. "For a couple of generations after that, the family was quite well-to-do. Wasn't cheap getting started with purebred dogs. No indeed. Nowadays, of course, it's hard for anyone to make ends meet."

Linnea felt guilty all over again for what her mother had done. She knew how many long hours Marsh worked between the store and the dogs. It amazed her that he'd been able to spare so much time to help her renovate the house.

"Marsh's got plans," Emma informed her.

She tried. She really tried not to ask, but the temptation was too great. And Emma clearly wanted to tell her more.

"What plans?"

"Wants to make the dogs turn a profit. He's already sold a few trained critters for a good sum, and then, of course, he started that business of giving rides the first winter he was home. Next step is to start racing the circuit. Win some prize money. That'll jack up the price of his dogs too."

"But if the family has been in the business so long—"

"Had to rebuild some. After Jen's father died there was just her and Marsh's mother to keep things going. No racing. No shows. No promotion. My great-nephew Chaz used to help them out, before he went away to college."

Emma chattered on, helping Linnea make more sandwiches while she talked. Without even asking, Linnea got the village's slant on Marsh's injury and disability pension.

He did have a hard time making ends meet, and yet he'd refused to take any pay for the work he'd done for her. He didn't want Denise's money, assuming Linnea could persuade her mother to part with it. He'd rather work eighty hours a week.

Pride, she decided. And stubbornness. He was not at all the sort of man she'd planned on falling for.

So why couldn't she stop following that suggestion made by the mystery writer who'd visited Cassie's class? She kept thinking "what if . . ." and dreaming up ways to start over again with Marsh. They ranged from cornering him in the storeroom at the market and seducing him into quivering submission, to climbing in through his bedroom window some dark night and seducing him into quivering—

Overactive imagination, she chided herself. Just like Cassie's.

She tuned in to Emma's account of another neighbor's problem with rats and quickly tuned out again after making an appropriately vague and encouraging sound.

No rats in her cellar. Only mice. Over the last week and a half she and Cassie had conducted a thorough search of Linnea's basement. They'd found no sign of any secret passage, hidden room, or bomb shelter.

Upstairs, they'd discovered that 3-D jigsaw puzzles were too darn hard for either of them to put together and switched to the one Cassie had of the turn-of-the-century train. They'd set it up at the Austins so that both Marsh and Linnea could help Cassie work on it . . . separately.

Just one more thing they'd never finish together? Linnea wondered. She was lecturing herself on the futility of pessimism when Cassie poked her head around the door frame.

"Emma! Linnea! Come quick! Bargain Bob found a hidden door when they cleared away the last of the barn. I think it's a secret tunnel!"

Linnea exchanged a startled glance with her companion. The sandwiches forgotten, they followed Cassie back outside.

"Couldn't be," Linnea murmured.

"Nothing's impossible," Emma replied.

By the time Marsh heard about it, Howard Dennison's bomb shelter had been completely excavated. Hours later, when he'd locked up the market and walked home, the party was over and everyone had left except Linnea and Cassie. They were both inside the shelter when he got there. He could hear their voices echoing inside the cavelike entrance.

"Hello?" he called. Part of him expected to hear Old Man Dennison's ghost yell back, "You go to the devil!"

The old barn hadn't been in good repair. The now gaping entrance had been hidden by fallen beams. There appeared to be a cement-block-lined passage, and it turned a corner while angling downward, belowground.

Not a good place for someone who was uncomfortable in small, enclosed areas. He remembered Linnea's words to Bargain Bob: *I can't think of anything worse than being trapped underground without air.* What on earth had possessed her to enter such a place?

The fact that others had gone before, he reminded himself. Everyone in town by now, except him. Picking up a flashlight someone had conveniently left near the opening, he started forward. His eyes widened when he came to the end of the tunnel. He'd never seen anything quite like this.

"Hey, big brother," Cassie greeted him. "Cool, huh?"

"All the comforts of home," Marsh said, noting two sets of bunk beds built along the walls.

The light from a large battery-powered lantern, placed on the floor in the middle of the room, revealed an area of no more than eight feet by twelve feet, jam-packed with survival gear. In addition to the bunks, there were rows of built-in cabinets loaded with supplies. He saw everything from eating utensils, paper plates, cups, and napkins to toilet tissue, paper towels, and soap.

He picked up a metal box and found within it openers for cans and bottles, a pocketknife, and a first-aid kit. Competing for space with can upon can of food were larger containers for garbage, toilet purposes, and to store human waste. Everything was labeled in large print.

"So, it was real, after all," he said to Linnea.

"Can't deny the obvious." Her smile seemed forced, and as he watched she shuddered.

"You okay?"

"This place gives me the willies," she confessed.

"You mean you're claustrophobic?"

"I'm not overly fond of enclosed places, but—"

"Shut your eyes for a minute." When she obeyed, he went on. "Imagine yourself at the ocean, with sea and sky spread out before you."

Her shaky laugh had him crossing the small space

and reaching for her. He wanted to take her in his arms, but he pulled back just in time. She opened her eyes and gave him a rueful look.

"Sorry. That made things worse. This place even has an underground smell to it. I can picture wide-open spaces, but I *know* I'm in a closed room surrounded by concrete blocks and dirt and rock."

"How can you not like enclosed places and still live in a city?"

"Cities aren't enclosed."

"I beg to differ. Subways. Elevators. Even the streets are claustrophobic. Think about it. Buildings on every side, right up to the sky. No way to get out. Like a long, long tunnel with no end. If you were truly claustrophobic, you wouldn't last five minutes without having to find a park."

"Is that how Boston affected you?"

"I'm not the one with claustrophobia."

"I only have a mild case. If that. If I was really phobic, I'd be incapacitated by my fear. And that's not what I meant about the willies." She pointed to a battery-operated radio with "Conelrad" frequencies marked. "This is like being in a time capsule, and it's not a time I'd have liked living in. My grandfather was apparently convinced that another world war was coming. What a terrible way to live."

Marsh didn't comment, but he did notice that the spare batteries meant to keep the radio going had leaked and were now useless. Seemed symbolic, somehow. The whole so-called cold war had been pretty futile.

Linnea moved away from him, poking into things on the shelves, as Cassie was already doing. "My grandfather was crazier than anybody thought."

"I'm not so sure. The way the world was then, he was acting sensibly. Today we have evacuation plans for areas around nuclear power plants. This isn't all that much different. Just a commonsense precaution."

He decided not to tell her about the popular Maine sentiment that called for blowing up the bridge between New Hampshire and Maine if the Boston area ever had to be evacuated northward.

"More like some of those survivalists," Linnea mused. "If my grandfather were alive today, he'd probably be stocking up on machine guns."

"Boy, is this going to make some story to tell the other kids at school," Cassie interrupted.

"What I did on my summer vacation?" Linnea asked.

"Yeah."

"I thought you hated the idea of school starting again," Marsh said.

"Not anymore. Can I bring some of my friends out to see this, Linnea?"

Linnea looked at him. "Your call, Marsh."

He didn't know whether to be pleased she'd deferred to him or irritated by yet another reminder that she was only here for the short haul. "If it's safe," he told his sister. "We don't want anyone to get accidentally locked in."

Cassie giggled. "I can think of a few I wouldn't—"

"Cass."

The warning note in his voice seemed to amuse her even more. She was chuckling as she went back to her explorations.

"Your grandfather put in a good supply of food," Marsh said to change the·subject. "A family of four could probably live down here for a couple of weeks."

"I wonder how long this stuff has been here?" Linnea pulled a tin of crackers down from a shelf and opened it. She dropped it a moment later.

The contents had been chewed. By mice, he assumed. Which meant this shelter wasn't as airtight as it should have been.

"I'd have to be starving before I'd eat that."

"The canned goods are probably unsafe by now," he agreed. "Dennison's been gone for fifteen years. Who knows how many years prior to that it was when he last stocked the shelves. There's bottled water, but I'm not sure I'd trust that, either. Not after all this time." He looked around for water purification tablets and found a bottle of household bleach instead.

"Bleach?" Linnea asked, seeing the direction of his gaze.

"Back before Austin's Crossing went on town water, every house had its own well. I can remember my grandfather dumping a bottle of bleach into ours every spring to kill off bacteria in the ground water. For a week afterward we'd smell like chlorine every time we came out of the shower. One time he put too much in and we all ended up with hair a shade lighter."

"You lived with your grandfather?"

"Yeah. After my father left, my mother and I

stayed on with his parents. She didn't leave till she married Cassie's father. I stayed behind then too."

He glanced toward Cassie, but she didn't seem to be listening. She was intent on digging something out from the back of a low shelf. Still, she was within earshot. He gave Linnea a warning glance.

"Relax," she whispered.

He wished he could. He hadn't anticipated the impact Linnea was having on him when they were confined this close together, even if it was inside a bomb shelter with his nine-year-old sister as unwitting chaperon.

Good thing Cassie was here, he told himself. Her presence was all that was keeping him from turning the incredible fantasy filling his mind into reality. He wanted nothing more than to lead Linnea over to one of those bunks and have his wicked way with her.

"Your eyes give you away," she murmured.

Startled, he met her steady gaze, and saw there an answering longing. Lust, he told himself. They had the hots for each other. That was all. Well, there was one sure way to cure *that* problem.

"I'll come back later," he whispered.

What was real was that Linnea would be in Austin's Crossing only a short while longer. He'd regret it for the rest of his life if he didn't find out what it would be like for them. There wasn't much risk, he told himself. They'd both know going in that there was an end in sight. They'd enjoy the time they had and with any luck they'd part friends.

"We do need to . . . talk," she said.

The response his eyes gave that comment made her blush. Marsh grinned.

"Hey, you guys!" Cassie yelled. "Look what I found!" She brushed off the knees of her jeans and stood, a triumphant look on her face and a metal box in her hands. "Treasure."

Waiting was hard.

More than an hour had passed since Marsh and Cassie had left to go back to their own house. Linnea had taken a shower and changed into a loose, comfortable velour robe and now sat alone in her newly decorated living room with the "treasure" on the coffee table in front of her.

She felt uncomfortably like the mythical Pandora. Would she come to regret her own curiosity?

There had been coins in the metal box. Old coins. Possibly valuable. Possibly not. But the true treasure had been hidden behind the metal box. The heavy plastic they'd been wrapped in had kept damage to a minimum. Her grandfather's journals were still legible.

She hesitated about reading them. So far, digging into her family's past had netted more negatives than positives. On the other hand, if she remembered the tale correctly, Pandora had managed to slam her box shut while hope was still inside. She'd kept that, even as she allowed sundry evils to escape into the world.

With a hand that shook just a little, Linnea picked up the first volume and opened it. Two hours later she hadn't read all the journals all the way through, but the small portion she'd sampled had helped her understand a great deal, not only about Howard Dennison, but about her own mother.

No wonder Denise wasn't much good at motherhood. She'd never had one of her own as a model. What she'd had was an eccentric, quarrelsome father. He'd loved her, in his own way, but she simply hadn't been as important to him as his pet projects, his pet peeves, or his cats.

Linnea couldn't help thinking how lucky Cassie was to have Marsh. And how much she was going to miss them both when she left Austin's Crossing. That made her more determined than ever to right old wrongs.

When Marsh knocked at the back door, she cut off whatever he'd been about to say with a rush of words of her own. "My mother owes your family the ten thousand dollars she extorted from your father, plus interest over a period of thirty years. I want to start a college fund for Cassie."

"No."

"Marsh—"

"We don't want any part of it. Denise earned her money."

That took a moment to sink in. "Are you saying she was paid for sex?"

He looked a little uncomfortable at her tone, but he shrugged and said, "If the shoe fits—"

"Oh, come on! She was a teenager. And unless I

miss my guess, she thought she was in love with the strong, silent type next door."

Taken aback, Marsh was at a loss for words, but only for a moment. He scowled fiercely. "He was married and way too old for her."

"He didn't exactly fight her off." She turned her back on him and returned to the living room, flinging herself down on the sofa where she'd been reading the journals.

She heard him lock the back door, then follow her. There was a distinctive cadence to his steps because of his injury, but Linnea found she rarely noticed his limp anymore. Too many other things about the man distracted her.

When the footfalls stopped, she knew he was standing by the pocket doors, staring at her, trying to figure her out. She wasn't sure what she was doing herself. Picking a fight to keep him at a distance? That was ridiculous when what she wanted most was to be in his arms. Maybe her grandfather wasn't the only one with a few screws loose.

"What is the point in discussing this now?" Marsh finally asked. "It happened a long time ago." He came into the room and gathered up the leather-bound journals, eight of them, each one covering several years, to clear a place for himself on the sofa.

"Exactly," she said. "A long time ago. It's past time to let go of it. If you won't let my mother make reparations to you, then let her help Cassie. She can afford it."

"What did she have on him?"

"What?"

He sat down beside her. Too close, yet too far away. "Why did he give her money? My mother already knew about the affair. What other secret could your mother possibly have threatened to expose?"

Linnea frowned. She hadn't really thought about that end of things. Hadn't wanted to, she supposed. In spite of the bitterness Denise had revealed when she spoke of being given money instead of love, Linnea had gotten the distinct sense that her mother also felt regret. Was it so impossible that her mother had loved Marsh's father? If he was anything like Marsh, she could understand both her mother's love and her frustration.

"Maybe he had feelings for her too," she suggested. "Maybe he wanted to help her get a fresh start."

"More likely he gave her the money to get her out of his life once and for all. Let's call it a payoff for his guilty conscience. She was only seventeen."

"I hadn't thought of that angle."

"You don't think like a cop."

"I'm not that cynical."

"There's no debt here, Linnea. Nothing. It's a closed case."

"And you and I?"

"We aren't our parents."

"No."

"What we do doesn't hurt anyone," he said, "won't break up any families."

"No."

He leaned toward her and caught her shoulders. As he pulled her close, with excruciating slowness, her surroundings blurred. Only Marsh was in focus, and all else, including everything that had happened in the past, melted away.

"Yes," she whispered.

The first kiss was arousing; the second was soul-shattering.

Fitting her body to his, Linnea knew she'd never felt more perfectly attuned to anyone. They moved as one, embracing, clinging, touching. His gentle hands sought her skin beneath the red velour, caressing her into a frenzy of need, a maelstrom of emotional longing.

This close to him, Linnea knew his reactions matched her own. She could feel the increased speed of his heart and the extent of his arousal against her thigh. She could taste his passion in every kiss.

Her own questing fingers sought the bottom edge of his cream-colored turtleneck, but his movements kept distracting her, breaking the concentration it took to maneuver the soft garment up his chest and over his head. When she managed to uncover the solid planes of his torso, she wanted nothing more than to taste his skin, to run the tip of her tongue over his flat, male nipples, to make him endure a bit of the delicious torture he was inflicting on her.

Breathing heavily, he caught her face, pressing her head to his still-covered shoulder. Her robe was open all down the front, baring her to his gaze. She made no pretense of modesty. She'd worn only the robe, hoping this would happen, hoping he wouldn't stop this time.

"Marsh," she whispered, a frisson of alarm disturbing the building passion. "There's no reason to stop."

"Only that I don't want our first time to be on your living-room sofa."

He held her still until he'd recovered enough to stand. Then he tugged her up with him, and before she could guess what he intended, he swept her into his arms.

For a moment he didn't move. She hoped the romantic gesture hadn't cost him too dearly. But she saw no pain reflected in his face when she tilted her head back to look at him. Only desire and tenderness.

Neither his weakened arm nor his limp slowed him down as he strode toward the stairs. She felt a wonderful sense of her own femininity as they climbed higher and higher. He made her feel fragile, delicate, as if she were the most precious thing in his life.

There would be no interruptions this time, she thought with a giddy sense of relief. The door was locked. They'd reached her attic room. He was placing her gently on her big Victorian bed and stripping off his turtleneck and jeans, taking his underwear with them.

Gloriously naked, he reached for her, divesting her of her robe in one smooth, sensual movement. He paused only long enough to don the protection he'd taken from the pocket of his jeans. Then he was beside her, taking her in his arms again, and kissing her into delirious oblivion.

She'd never felt so free, never been so adventurous. His murmured praises, his enticing touches, provoked a matching enthusiasm in her. She was as bold as he, learning his body as he learned hers. And when the moment came to join together, they matched as if they'd been created just for each other.

Two halves made whole.

Two souls soared together. Two bodies caught the ancient rhythms of love and in perfect harmony dissolved into the ultimate ecstasy.

"I didn't know it could be that good," Linnea whispered when she'd caught her breath again.

"I didn't either," he confessed.

And when they'd recovered sufficiently, to their amazement and delight, they discovered that it could be "that good" more than once.

TEN

"You do realize you're hanging that wallpaper upside down?" Marsh said as he entered the upstairs bedroom.

"No I'm not."

"Look again." He commandeered the piece she'd been about to slather with wallpaper paste and turned it around. "What do you see?"

Linnea blinked. One moment she saw only a geometrical design; the next, she saw what he had—lovebirds billing and cooing inside a decorative border. "Good grief. It's like one of those drawings where you see faces if you look at it one way and a vase if you look another."

"You really didn't notice before?"

"No, I really didn't notice before." She glanced at the two walls she'd already papered. "Do you think anyone will? I mean, if it isn't pointed out . . ."

"If the people who buy this house don't like it, they can put up their own wallpaper."

He meant to be reassuring, she was certain, but his words had a different effect. Suddenly she felt very sad. She didn't want to sell this house. Or leave Austin's Crossing. Or leave Marsh.

She almost told him so, but chickened out at the last second. As he dropped the wallpaper and walked toward her, she could smell the musky aftershave he was wearing. Musk? He'd changed scents, abandoning his spicy old standby.

Unaccountably annoyed, Linnea backed away. She knew why he was there, in the middle of the afternoon. The amorous gleam in his eyes would have told her that even if she wasn't being smothered by what he obviously thought was a sexy scent. He'd asked Emma to spell him at the store, probably on the pretext of "helping" his neighbor with her renovations, when all he'd ever intended was to coax her back into bed.

She'd really resent his attitude, she thought, if she'd ever given him any indication that she wanted more than great sex from him. He didn't have a clue how she really felt. How could he, when even now she was succumbing to his overwhelmingly masculine lure? Achieving his goal wasn't going to take much coaxing. She was putty in his talented hands and he knew it.

Linnea repressed a sigh. Marsh saw their relationship as a short-term affair, mutually satisfying but doomed to end when she left Austin's Crossing.

Enjoy what you have, she told herself. These last two weeks, with Marsh in her bed every night and during a few special afternoons, too, had been blissful beyond belief. There was no reason she shouldn't enjoy the weeks ahead just as much.

Except that each day would bring her closer to the time when she'd leave Austin's Crossing, and Marsh, forever.

Spurred on by discontent, she summoned up a modicum of resistance. Wrinkling her nose in exaggerated distaste, she took him to task for his heavy-handed seduction technique. "Go back to the other brand, Marsh," she drawled in a fair imitation of his own rural twang. "Musk doesn't do a thing for me."

Instead of taking offense, he chuckled. "Anyone ever tell you you're cute when you're trying to be ornery?"

"Anyone ever tell you that you can be a real jerk sometimes?"

He ignored the insult and leaned closer, nuzzling the nape of her neck. "Want to know what my favorite perfume is? The one I've fantasized about smelling on you?"

"Not particularly. And stop trying to distract me. I want to finish papering this room before the wallpaper paste all dries up."

"Cinnamon."

That startled her enough that she stopped struggling. "Cinnamon?"

"Cinnamon. It's a real turn-on."

"Fine. Let me finish my work and I'll drive to the Maine Mall and try to buy cinnamon perfume."

"Cinnamon, the spice. You have it in your kitchen. Picture this, Linnea—cinnamon dabbed all over you. Maybe even sprinkled into the water in the claw-footed tub. I could run the water for you while you finish up here. Surely after all this hard work you'll want a nice relaxing bath?"

"Marsh!" She shouldn't be shocked. She certainly wasn't offended. But a trembling had started in her lower limbs and was slowly encompassing her entire body.

"Deal?"

Struggling for self-possession, she stepped out of his embrace. "One condition." She grinned at him, entering into his fantasy in spite of herself. "You have to join me."

"I planned to."

"But you have to go home and take a shower first. Get rid of every bit of that awful musk scent. You see . . ." She ran one finger up over his shoulder and across his jaw. "I'm rather fond of spices myself."

In the depths of his heated gaze she saw a fire kindling, ready to burst into flame. He reached for her but she danced away.

"Got to finish work first," she said. "Maybe you should make that shower a cold one."

"Linnea." His voice was dark and husky, sending a sensual shiver through her.

"One more thing, Marsh. Leave your hair loose. I love long hair on a man." His was long and wavy, but she rarely had a chance to enjoy it since he customarily wore it dragged back into that queue.

"I'm partial to long hair on a woman," he countered, "but I'm getting used to yours."

Taken aback, she lifted one hand to touch her short-cropped locks. "Hey. Broaden your horizons, country boy."

"For you, city girl, anything."

He'd been prowling steadily closer, and she was beginning to doubt she'd get her paper hung that afternoon, when something outside caught his attention, distracting him from his purpose. A frown darkening his features, he strode to the window, lifted the sheer curtains she'd just hung, and peered out through the sparkling-clean glass.

"What is it, Marsh?"

"Cassie and two of her school friends. They're headed for the bomb shelter. Did you give her permission to go in there?"

"Of course not. And ever since you discovered that the door catch is faulty and the ventilation system doesn't work properly, I've kept it padlocked." In what Marsh had called the worst-case scenario, a child or animal could be trapped inside what was, in essence, an oversized refrigerator.

"Where did you put the key?"

"On the rack inside the back door." She joined him at the window, the hairs on the back of her neck prickling as she watched his sister's stealthy progress across her backyard. Cassie was up to no good.

"Let's let this play out," he said grimly. "She

needs to learn a lesson. I'll close the door myself once she's inside."

"That's cruel, Marsh." And dangerous. "She's going to think she's trapped in there."

"I don't think anything less is going to make an impression on her."

Linnea couldn't let him go through with his plan, though. She couldn't tolerate the thought of Cassie and her friends in a panic, convinced their air was running out. Let him deal with the girl's disobedience some other way. Without another word she turned and started for the door, intending to descend the stairs and catch Cassie in the act of filching the key.

Marsh caught her arm before she'd gone two steps. "My call, Linnea."

She glared over her shoulder at him. "Not when you're wrong."

"Even then. My sister. My problem." But she had, she could see, made him stop and think. "I'll just talk to her," he promised, "but I need to get down there. To set those girls straight."

"Come back when things are settled," she said. "I'll be waiting to hear what happened."

"Keep the water hot," he joked, but his heart was no longer in it.

There goes that romantic interlude, she thought glumly as she watched him descend her front staircase.

She returned to her papering. Better to keep busy and hold worry at bay. But as time passed and Marsh did not return, she had more and more difficulty blocking out her concern about what was going on at the shelter.

And then a truly terrible thought struck her. What if, somehow, they'd all gotten trapped in there? Fear gave wings to her feet as she hurtled down the stairs. She was halfway to the back door when it opened to admit Marsh.

One look at his face told her he'd had a rough time of it. He sank into a kitchen chair, just shaking his head and looking like he badly needed a friend.

With swift efficiency, Linnea made coffee, then sat down opposite him with her own steaming mug. "What happened?" she asked when he still didn't volunteer anything. "Are the girls all right?"

"They weren't exploring." He ran agitated fingers through his hair, finally pulling it free of the queue. He hardly seemed aware of what he was doing. He certainly wasn't trying to seduce her anymore.

"All right, I'll bite. What were they doing?" A glance at the key rack told her the key to the shelter was missing. "They did open it up, right?"

"Right. I can't believe this. I thought Cassie had more sense. Of all the irresponsible, reckless, *stupid* things to do."

"Ah, Marsh? A few specifics, please? It's hard to know what you're talking about when I wasn't there."

He took a restorative sip of coffee first, then looked up. His eyes were filled with confusion and disappointment as they met hers. "Cassie and her best friend, Chloe, were going to spring a trap on their other 'friend' Jane. They actually intended to lock her in, though they swore they were going to let her out again before the air ran out."

"But why? What did this Jane do to them?"

"It seems she deliberately rode her bike straight at Chloe, stopping only a centimeter short of running her down. For fun. To scare her. Cassie decided Jane deserved a good scare in return. What am I going to do with her, Linnea?"

"What have you done so far?"

"Told her she could have killed that little girl with her carelessness. I think I made an impression on her, but I'm not sure."

Linnea reached across the table to place her hand over Marsh's. "It isn't as if she's embarking on a life of crime, Marsh. It was a prank. Ill thought out, true, but not so very terrible as these things go. She knew she had to let Jane out quickly. She just intended to scare her." Linnea hesitated, then added, "The same exact thing you considered doing to her."

He had the grace to look embarrassed.

"Look, Marsh, I know you're appalled by what almost happened, and disappointed in Cassie, but don't make too much of it. She made a mistake in judgment. I'm sure she knows that now. Don't beat yourself up over it."

"And Cassie? What do I do with her?"

"Well, I suppose the old country way would be a trip to the woodshed."

"Not exactly politically correct in the nineties."

"What, then?"

"Would you talk to her?"

Linnea promised she would, and she could practically see the heavy weight lift from Marsh's shoulders. Knowing she'd helped him gave her a kind of contentment that had been rare in her life. She'd been looking forward to cinnamon and a tryst in the claw-footed tub, but this moment was far more special.

Maybe there was hope for her and Marsh, after all.

The woman sleeping beside him was everything he'd ever wanted, Marsh thought, and he was deluding himself if he believed he'd have her for long. She was going to leave him. If he had any sense, he'd break it off with her himself, before she got around to it.

He brushed a stray strand of hair away from her perfect mouth and fought the urge to wake her, to make love to her again until they were both too exhausted to think.

Thinking was the problem.

He wished he could just relax and enjoy what they had together as long as it lasted.

No chance, though.

Linnea had become way too important to him. As hard as he'd been trying to avoid an emotional involvement, he knew he was but a hairsbreadth away from being in love with her.

That knowledge forced him from her bed before she woke. Loving Linnea was a sure route to heartbreak. She was a city girl. Sooner or later that siren call would lure her back. Hell, why shouldn't it? It had pulled everyone he'd ever loved away from him, starting with Linnea's mother.

He told himself he had to be getting back home anyway. Though half the town probably had a good idea what was going on between him and Linnea, they'd been careful not to flaunt their relationship, especially around Cassie.

It hardly set a good example for a young girl. Marsh was just glad she was only nine. Hopefully she hadn't gotten interested in the birds and the bees yet.

Bad enough she got up to the things she did. He still shuddered every time he thought of the bomb-shelter incident, and that had taken place nearly three weeks ago. After a long private chat with Linnea, however, Cassie had apologized to Jane and to Marsh. Whatever Linnea had said to her had made a deep impression.

Despite that rocky start, Cassie had taken to school like a duck to water, and she barely had any time for the adults in her life. She was so busy with her friends that it took the combined efforts of Jen, Marsh, and Linnea just to drive her to all the extracurricular activities she'd gotten involved in. Marsh no longer had to worry that his kid sister would be devastated when Linnea left town. No, he was the only one in danger of that.

Linnea sighed and rolled over. He held his breath, but she didn't wake. Quietly, he reached for his shirt, but he continued to stare at the woman in the bed as he dressed.

For weeks now, ever since they'd first made love,

he had let things drift. Each time, making love with her had been as fulfilling, as exciting, as that first mind-boggling encounter. For a while he was always able to forget that their future had already been decided.

When her four months were up, only another month from now, she'd sell this house and leave. That was what he'd wanted. He ought to want it still. After all, she'd be miserable if she stayed, and that would mean she'd end up making his life miserable, as well.

Suppose he were fool enough to marry her? A year or two down the road she'd get tired of the rural solitude. She'd head for bright city lights. And she might try to take Cassie with her.

No.

He couldn't allow that to happen.

Not even great sex was worth that price.

By the time he'd finished dressing and gone downstairs, Marsh realized that the only solution was to put a little distance between himself and Linnea. Even though an affair was what he'd thought he wanted, he wasn't sure he could handle it any longer. Someway, somehow, he had to fight harder against falling in love. If he didn't, certain disaster loomed ahead.

"Ready to go?" Linnea asked.

Marsh's answer was more grunt than word.

She turned away from the sink and went over to him, putting her arms around him and kissing him square on the lips. "Bad day at the office?" she teased.

A reluctant smile answered her. It was eight in the morning. In order to accompany Cassie's class on a field trip, he'd taken the day off from the store. He had, however, been up early to work with the dogs.

"Nap on the way there and I'll drive," she suggested. Somehow, she'd been recruited as a chaperon too. She was secretly very pleased and honored to have been asked.

She could tell Marsh tried, but he couldn't hang on to his taciturn attitude. Still, Linnea had sensed something bothering him for the last week, ever since the morning when she'd awakened to find him gone without a word of farewell. That had broken the pattern they'd set over the course of the previous weeks, the affectionate cuddling after they made love, the tender good-byes before he went home in dawn's early light.

He was afraid. It didn't take a shrink to figure that much out.

So was she.

They made the drive to the living-history center, following the school bus, in relative silence. "Have you been here before?" Linnea finally asked.

"Every kid in the state has been here or to Norlands. And a lot of the teachers come and stay a week, living in character and in costume the entire time."

Her own recent interest in history, at least in that of the Dennisons and Austins, made Linnea curious enough to stick around when her young charges were herded into a tent to participate in a typical lesson at a school of the 1850s. A sheaf of flyers held down by a rock announced that the schoolhouse that had been used before had been destroyed by fire a month earlier. Donations were being solicited in order to build a replica. In the interim, the costumed teacher had to make do with holding classes under canvas.

Linnea read the fund-raising information twice, then looked around for Marsh, but he was nowhere in sight. He had said something about watching the team of oxen at work. With a shrug, she proceeded on her own. Finding the director of the living-history center wasn't hard.

"What about replacing your schoolhouse with another?" she asked. "Moving a replacement building to the site instead of building a reproduction? Surely there must be some available in neighboring towns." Like Austin's Crossing.

The director shook his head. "Most towns turn their old schools into tourist information centers or convert them for office space."

"I may know an exception."

"I'm all ears," the director said.

Linnea didn't plan on keeping her meddling secret from Marsh, but they ended up giving one of the parents a lift home and she was loath to raise the subject of the schoolhouse lot with a stranger in the car. Once they reached Austin's Crossing, there was no opportunity, either. Marsh was anxious to get to the store, to make sure there hadn't been any problems in his absence.

That evening, Linnea found herself procrastinating. She was no longer sure how Marsh would react to her news. She told herself she'd lead up to the subject gradually. It wasn't her fault that the living-history center had already started negotiations to acquire the building, that matters were moving much more swiftly than she'd anticipated. If Marsh didn't like the idea, it was already too late to stop the events she'd put in motion.

"I wish we could use your outdoor fireplace to cook the burgers," she said, avoiding dangerous waters entirely.

She missed summer now that the evenings were getting so much shorter. It was the third week in October, almost time to set the clocks back, and darkness already fell far too early to suit her. She'd been spoiled by a gorgeous Indian summer and all that foliage. Even though she was looking forward to the first snowfall, she wasn't keen to experience dusk before four o'clock every afternoon.

"That fireplace will be a memory soon." The morose note in his voice surprised her out of her ruminations.

"What are you talking about?"

"The fireplace, which my great-grandfather built, is in the process of slipping down the bank. It'll end up in the river one of these days."

"Why don't you dismantle it and reassemble it farther back from the edge?" An opening to bring up the subject of the schoolhouse seemed to have fallen into her lap.

"Erosion is inevitable. It would catch up eventually."

She wondered why he was being so negative tonight. She was tempted to blame the season, the early dusk and all that. Other than regretting the lack of sunshine, she'd never been much affected by it herself, but she supposed Marsh might be.

"In the meantime we still have the use of the fireplace," she reminded him. "Look at the bright side, Marsh."

"I'm just being realistic."

"If you say so."

"And I'm not all that fond of change. It usually isn't for the good."

"You are such a pessimist," she muttered under her breath as she went back to fixing supper. Maybe this wasn't the time to tell him about the lot on the other side of his house, after all.

"And you're an optimist," he said glumly. "Oil and water."

"What?"

"Don't mix."

Linnea had been wary all along of her growing emotional involvement with Marsh, but his attitude this evening really made her nervous. He was being very quick to assume they had no future together.

Sighing, she turned back to her cooking. The longer she lived in Austin's Crossing, the less desire she felt to return to the high-pressure life of a corporate executive. Lately she'd begun to consider the possibility of living here permanently. The biggest thing holding her back was her inability to figure out a way to make ends meet if she did so.

The idea of change *was* scary, she silently acknowledged. But that didn't mean a person stayed stuck in a rut just to avoid it.

"Did you have a lot of doubts about staying when you first came home?" she asked Marsh.

"No."

And that, she knew, was all he'd say on the subject if she didn't push him. Marsh didn't like to talk about the past.

"Jen says you came back for Cassie's sake."

"Jen talks too much."

"Did you want to come back?"

His laugh was harsh. "What choice did I have? I was shot about a year before my mother died."

"What took you a year?"

"Physical therapy, mostly. Subject closed, Linnea."

She couldn't let it drop, though. "You might have stayed in the city. Sold the house here."

Anger flared in his eyes, then was gone. "I wanted to come back. Okay? And I have no regrets, except that I ever left in the first place."

There was so much bitterness in his voice, bitterness that Linnea was at a loss to understand. He belonged here. He was making it here. He loved his family and he loved training the dogs. The only thing in his life that he didn't love was her.

Don't think like that, she told herself.

Whatever decision she made, to go or to stay, couldn't depend solely upon Marsh Austin. She was responsible for her own happiness.

She began again as she served up their simple meal of burgers and fries. "I've been rereading my grandfather's journals," she said.

Marsh didn't say anything, just waited for her to go on.

"For all his . . . eccentricities, I'm beginning to feel he and I have a lot in common. I'm certainly feeling more empathy toward him than I ever did toward my mother."

"They never got along."

"Neither do she and I. I wish I'd known him."

"Might not have liked him much."

"And maybe I'd have adored him." She glanced around the kitchen, gleaming now with freshly painted cabinets and cheerful wallpaper, and with framed prints of various herbs decorating the walls. "I love his house."

The house was almost complete. Unfortunately, she was also almost out of money. And the people who'd sublet her condo were pressuring her. They wanted to buy it from her. She had to give them an answer soon.

"There are a lot of nice things about small-town life," she went on. "I think I've begun to prefer it to living in a big, impersonal city."

"You'll readjust."

"I'm not sure I want to."

He put his fork down and stared hard at her. "Don't get ideas, Linnea. You haven't spent a winter in Maine. You wouldn't like it."

"I wish everyone would stop telling me what I'll

like and won't like. You and my mother, Marsh, have more in common than you know."

"Appalling thought."

"Would you hate it that much if I stayed longer?"

"I think it would . . . complicate things."

"I'm not trying to pressure you into marrying me, Marsh." Exasperated, she rose and started clearing away the half-eaten meal.

"Whoa, there."

"And I'm not one of your dogs!"

"You're snapping at me like one." His arms came around her waist, and he nuzzled the back of her neck. "Sweetheart, let's not quarrel. Let's enjoy the fact that you're here now and let tomorrow take care of itself."

The surge of desire she felt, that she always felt when she was this close to him, temporarily overcame her doubts. He was right about one thing. What they had together today was precious, and should be savored.

It was still too early to tell him that in addition to the fact that she'd fallen in love with this house, she'd gone and fallen in love with him.

What they'd both thought was going to be a brief, mutually satisfying affair had turned into much, much more.

ELEVEN

Linnea's renovations were finished.

Marsh gave the old Dennison house a good hard look one crisp mid-November morning. He was heading to work at the market, but he slowed his steps as he passed by Linnea's place and really studied the facade, impressed by what she'd accomplished. The exterior was white, with dark blue shutters to match the front door and the tile on the roof.

He had to hand it to her. She had determination. Even with the additional work she'd decided to do only a few weeks earlier, furnishing as well as decorating each of the three large bedrooms on the second floor, everything on her agenda had been completed before her self-imposed four-month deadline. Tomorrow, he figured, she'd put up a "For Sale" sign. She had no reason to stay longer.

It was then he noticed that a sign was already affixed to the railing of her front porch. Marsh detoured closer. Something didn't seem quite right about that sign.

"What the hell?" He blinked and looked again, trying to take in the implications. The neat black letters on the oval board spelled out BRYAN'S BED-AND-BREAKFAST.

"Like it?" Linnea came out onto the porch, her lips curved in a tremulous smile.

There were at least a dozen comments he might have made, none of them encouraging. He said the first thing that came into his mind. "Since when do you know anything about running a B&B?"

"I didn't know anything about renovating a house four months ago. What's your point?"

"You can't stay here." With a tug, he loosened the collar of his flannel shirt, wondering why he was suddenly finding it so difficult to breathe.

"Of course I can stay."

"Why prolong this? You'll leave eventually."

He could sense that his sharp words hurt her, but he would not, could not call them back. When she turned and went inside, he followed her through the front door. Had it only been a few hours since he'd left though the back? She might have warned him what she was planning. Irritated, he scowled at her. She glowered right back.

"Are you sure you want to come through the courting door?" she asked him, throwing back at him the taunt he'd uttered months before. "Someone might think you've got honorable intentions."

A part of him wished that really were possible, but

he'd learned a long time ago not to cry for the moon. "Think, Linnea. This isn't for you. Before you came here, you'd had a setback in your career. Your self-confidence had taken a beating. Maybe you were even afraid you'd fail to find a new job. You came here to regroup, to hide out."

"I came here to sell my grandfather's house."

"Exactly. And things ended up taking a little longer than you'd planned. But you know you miss your old life. You can't linger here forever. Hell, you couldn't stay away from the city even this long. You've made two trips away from here in just the last month."

"Of course I did. To sign the papers to sell my condo to the people who have been subletting it. And to make arrangements with my mother's friend Bernie to pick up his Mustang."

"You sold your car?" Although she'd never explained why, he knew that Mustang meant a lot to her.

"I sold my car." A small, enigmatic smile danced across her features and then was gone. "I didn't need it anymore."

"You need some vehicle to get around. We don't exactly have much in the way of public transportation in Austin's Crossing."

She shrugged, unconcerned. "Maybe I'll pick up a used truck or something later, but there's no rush. With your store right down the street, all the basic necessities are within walking distance."

"You'll have cabin fever inside of a week once the snow comes."

"Not with paying guests in the house. Then, too,

I've no doubt that one of my neighbors will take pity on me and offer to drive me to the big city of New Portsmouth if I really crave a night on the town. I doubt I'll get that stir-crazy. There's a great deal of work involved in running a successful B&B, you know."

"How much are you really going to know about your prospective guests?" he demanded. She hadn't thought this through. She couldn't have.

"That a lot of them are your customers too."

"What?"

"You heard me. The bookings I've already made are all people coming to go on dogsled rides. Quite a good number too. This could work out very well for both of us, Marsh. If they have a nice place to stay right in your backyard, so to speak, they're likely to stick around longer and pay for more trips. At twenty dollars a pop for adults and ten for kids, you'll soon be raking in the money."

"They can stay at the motel in New Portsmouth. It's been good enough for folks so far."

She just gave him a look, and he quickly dropped that subject.

There was only one way she could have gotten that business, he thought. Jen did the bookings for the dogsled rides. She'd conspired with Linnea to set this up. Jen thought she was doing it for his own good, he was sure, but he couldn't help the acute sense of betrayal that swept over him. He'd thought he could trust Aunt Jen. At least she'd never gone off and left him.

"You can sell this place now for enough to bankroll your job search," he said aloud.

"I don't need to look for a job anymore. I have one."

"You have no experience. You'll miss your old career, your old friends."

"I've already made new friends and I wasn't all that happy in my old career."

"And this one? In a year or two, when it starts to get boring? Or if there aren't enough customers to pay the bills? Self-employed people go bankrupt every year. Believe me, I know the statistics."

"Are you going to tell me I'll miss company insurance policies too? And retirement benefits? I graduated from one of the best business colleges in the country, Marsh. I know what I'm doing."

The more she argued, the more determined he became. He needed to convince her to end this foolishness and leave. Make a clean break.

He clamped down hard on the hope that kept fluttering deep in his heart. This was no time to show weakness. He knew he was right. If he let himself believe she meant what she said, they'd both end up getting hurt. Maybe not this month. Maybe not even this year. But eventually, inevitably . . . The best thing he could do for the woman he loved was urge her to go.

Loved?

Well, hell.

That was the problem, wasn't it? In spite of his best effort, he'd slipped over the line. It was a waste of time to try to deny the truth to himself. But he could harden his resolve. For both their sakes.

"You won't be happy here," he said.

"I've been *very* happy here for four months."

"If you're hoping I'll change my mind and ask you to marry me, you can forget it."

Her remarkable aquamarine eyes first widened, then narrowed angrily at his words. "Just for curiosity's sake, exactly what makes you think I'd be such a dreadful wife? You can't deny we've got a satisfying physical relationship."

The taunting words provoked him. He responded without thinking through what he was saying. "Maybe that's exactly why I don't want to marry you. I've got Cassie to think of. Some role model you'd be."

For a moment he thought she was going to hit him. "I'm a bad example?" she asked in a voice that was far too quiet.

"Family values are important. A young girl needs to—"

"You bastard!" She flew at him, but stopped just short of a collision. Glaring at him, her fists clenched at her sides, she berated him, her voice rising. "Where do you come off throwing around an outdated double standard like that? I haven't been alone in that bed, you know."

"Linnea—" Too late, Marsh realized just how cruel his words had been.

"Loving you doesn't exactly make me promiscuous."

"I wasn't the first."

She took the verbal blow hard, flinching and retreating a few steps. Her voice dropped to a lower register. "I'm not even going to respond to that." Her resolution didn't last. Turning away from him, throwing her hands up in disgust, she spat out a single word, making it an expletive. "Men!"

"I'm thinking of Cassie," he said in an admittedly weak defense. "If you didn't feel you had to save yourself for the right man, wait for the real thing, she's not going to see any point in doing so, either."

"First of all, it's none of her business what I did before I met you. And none of your business, either. And in the second place, I *thought* I had found the real thing with you." Abruptly, she swung around to face him again. Her voice shook a little, but she met and held his gaze. "I love you, Marshall Austin, but you'll never believe that, will you? You'll just say I'm deluding myself, or maybe playing some kind of sick city-girl game."

She loved him? She'd never come right out and said so before. After one last searching look into clear aquamarine depths, he broke eye contact.

Gritting his teeth to keep his own feelings in, he did just as she'd predicted, told himself she only thought she was in love with him. He was a passing fancy, nothing more.

"I'm concerned about Cassie," he said again. He was too. "Things are calm now, but last summer, right after you first arrived on the scene, my sister started acting up, sulking when she didn't get enough attention. She could have done serious harm with that prank in the bomb shelter. Who knows what she'll do now if she doesn't get her way? After all, with you right next door to run to . . ."

"That's unfair." She put one hand on his forearm, but he shook it off.

"Whoever said life was fair?"

She did hit him then, a hard, frustrated rap with her fist to his shoulder. "Will you listen to yourself?"

He had been, and he didn't like what he was hearing. But he couldn't seem to stop himself from blundering on. "You'll leave eventually. It would be best for all concerned if you left now."

Easier to bear.

Even if it did break his heart.

"You can't bring yourself to trust me, can you?" she asked. "You won't let yourself believe I love you, or that I mean to stay. Which, incidentally, is a separate issue entirely."

A suspicious moistness shimmered in her eyes, but no tears fell. The anguish he saw as he gazed into her stricken face nearly tore him apart. He wanted to confess that he loved her, that he wanted her to stay more than he wanted his next breath, but at the same time he had to urge her to leave, before they hurt each other even more.

"Linnea—"

"No. You've made yourself clear. Well, surprise! You're the one who's leaving, Marsh." She stuck out one hand, palm up. "I want your key back and then I want you out of my house. I can't continue in a sexual relationship with someone who doesn't believe a word I say."

"So that's it then." He fished the key out of his pocket, fumbling slightly, and handed it over.

He told himself it would only be a matter of days before she took down the bed-and-breakfast sign and put up one that said FOR SALE. Then she'd be gone. Out of his life. Out of Cassie's life.

That was for the best.

But he'd never felt so empty, so lifeless, as he did when he walked away from Linnea's house that morning. It was as if he'd left his heart behind with her.

Linnea fought against the tears, but her effort was futile. They streamed unchecked down her face. She hadn't been able to keep herself from falling in love with Marsh, so it only made sense she wouldn't be able to control her emotions now.

The irony was that she was almost certain Marsh loved her in return. He just wouldn't admit it. He had to be the most pigheaded man she'd ever met.

Well, she was stubborn too. And she'd made her stand. She was open for business.

She felt a sudden desire, which she barely contained, to go over to the Austins' backyard and kick that stone fireplace the rest of the way down the bank.

Change could be good, dammit!

Eventually, her tears subsided. If Marsh refused to believe her commitment would last, there wasn't

much she could do about it—except to go on as she'd
started.

She'd keep fighting her own doubts too. Lord
knew, she had plenty of those. What if he couldn't let
go of his biases? What if he was still confusing her
with her mother, even though he'd said often enough
that he wasn't? Maybe, subconsciously, he blamed her
for what Denise had done to break up his parents'
marriage.

No. No, she couldn't think like that. One pessimist in this relationship was quite enough. She'd just
have to convince Marsh he was wrong. Force him to
admit that they were meant to be together and that
she belonged here in Austin's Crossing. She was sure
she could stick it out until he came to his senses.

With plenty of work to do to get ready for her first
guests, Linnea put aside her lingering fears for the rest
of the day. But when it came time to go to bed, alone
for the first time in weeks, niggling doubts surfaced to
torment her.

Why on earth had she demanded his key back?
Out of hurt, she'd cut off any easy way for him to
apologize. Not that she expected he'd just ignore their
quarrel and try to take up where they'd left off, but if
he were to appear at the foot of her bed right
now . . .

She sighed and tried to get comfortable. They
needed some time apart to sort things out. What was
that old saw about absence making the heart grow
fonder? Of course, he wouldn't exactly be absent.
He'd be right next door.

Linnea couldn't decide whether she felt encouraged or dismayed by that fact, and tried to turn her thoughts to something else. Unfortunately, the subject her mind came up with was equally worrisome.

Had Marsh been right? Was she so determined to stay in Austin's Crossing because she was afraid to fail again in the urban business world?

She closed her eyes tightly and pulled the covers up to her chin. *I am not running away*, she told herself firmly. *I'm coming home.*

A week later Linnea was curled up on the window seat in the living room, staring morosely out at the gently falling snowflakes. She'd wanted to share the first snow of the season with Marsh. It saddened her that she couldn't.

A wry smile flickered across her lips. Well, she could. The market was less than a five-minute walk away. He could scarcely hide from her in a village this small. But he'd made it clear he didn't want any more to do with her, and she'd be damned if she'd chase after him like some desperate spinster.

In all the long days and longer nights since she'd thrown him out of her house, she'd been unable to think of any way to convince him her feelings for him were genuine. Truthfully, it amazed her that they still were, considering how irritated she was at him for the absurd and insulting things he'd said to her that day. That was love for you. Illogical. Because she did love him, she could forgive him everything.

Now all she had to do was change his mind about her.

Defiantly, she had opened her bed-and-breakfast. She'd had two paying customers just the night before. Three more were coming in for the weekend. She was going to stay in Austin's Crossing, even if Marsh continued to push her away until he'd killed every gentle feeling they had for each other.

The sound of a large truck's backup siren brought her to her feet. No more time to feel sorry for herself. She and Jen had agreed to meet out front to watch them move the old schoolhouse away. From the sound of it, the action was about to begin.

Marsh still had no inkling that she was the one who'd started the ball rolling, making it possible for him to buy the property on the far side of his lot. Jen said he'd been floored when one of the New Portsmouth selectmen called to tell him the news. Once the schoolhouse was gone, the land was his for a token payment. And future taxes, of course. The parcel was too small and too close to the river for anyone to build on. The town was glad to get anything at all for it.

The ramp Marsh had built for Jen's wheelchair allowed her to reach the driveway, and from there she had clear sailing to the road. A little snow didn't deter her at all. In fact, she seemed as delighted as a child by the flakes landing on her hair and nose.

"We'll be out in the sleds soon," she called to Linnea, and something in her voice made Linnea think Jen would understand what the Mustang had meant to her. "I wish you'd let me tell Marsh you had a hand in this." Jen gestured toward the schoolhouse as it was eased off its foundation.

"He'd probably just think we were conspiring against him. Again."

Jen snorted. "Honestly. It is so obvious that you two are meant for each other. If you hadn't been, why would he have spent the last couple of months sneaking over to your place every night?"

"You know you weren't supposed to notice," Linnea chided her. "And God forbid Cassie should find out."

"Cassie is the one who told me," Jen said. "And she thinks the two of you ought to get married and have babies. The only reason she hasn't said so to Marsh is because I made her promise not to. The man has been worse than a dog with a sore paw since you kicked him out of your bed."

"He knows where I am, but I'm not holding my breath, waiting for him to turn up on my doorstep."

"Let's hope he just needs a little time to come to his senses."

"Given Marsh's stubbornness, I could be living next door to him ten years from now and he'd still think I was on the verge of running back to the city."

"Impossible man!"

They watched as the schoolhouse was successfully loaded up and carted away. Then Linnea pushed Jen back into the house.

"In the past few weeks," Linnea said, "I've spent an extraordinary amount of time following some advice Cassie told me a visiting mystery writer gave her class last year. I ask myself what if. What if Marsh really loves me? And then I think, what if he really doesn't and never did? I don't have any answers, but I have realized one thing. Either way, I still want to stay here. I belong in Austin's Crossing now."

"It *is* right for you," Jen agreed. "Marsh or no Marsh."

With Marsh, Linnea thought, it would be perfection.

It was a painful pleasure to be this close to Linnea again. Marsh didn't know whether to be angry or grateful that Aunt Jen had insisted Linnea share Thanksgiving dinner with them. He was definitely frustrated. The air was redolent with the smell of fresh-baked apple pie . . . and cinnamon.

Part of him was surprised she was still around. On the other hand, it hadn't been that long since she'd finished the house. Even if she'd put up a "For Sale" sign, it would take a while to sell.

There was no "For Sale" sign, though. Just the one indicating the place was a B&B. And she'd had two single men staying with her all last week. He didn't like *that* at all.

Next week, she'd have some of his customers in her guest rooms. He wasn't sure how he felt about the prospect. One thing was certain. He wasn't going to be able to ignore for much longer the fact that Linnea Bryan was still living right next door to him.

It was all but impossible now. Aunt Jen talked

about Linnea. Cassie talked about Linnea. Emma talked about Linnea. Now perfect strangers would be talking about Linnea as he headed off into the wilderness with them.

No one seemed to mind Marsh's silence during the meal. Jen told Linnea about the crossword puzzles she was attempting to create to sell to the local, twice-weekly county newspaper. Cassie chattered away about school and her friend Chloe. Then, out of the blue, she asked Linnea why she wasn't spending this quintessentially family holiday with her parents.

"My mother and I don't get along," Linnea answered, "and I never did see much of my father."

"I don't see much of my father, either," Cassie said.

"I visit mine once or twice a year," Linnea elaborated. "We aren't close, but I don't want to lose touch with him entirely."

The moment the words were out, she seemed to realize how Cassie might take them. She met Marsh's worried gaze with an alarmed look of her own. They both waited with bated breath.

"Can I go visit my father?" Cassie asked Marsh.

"I'm not sure where he is," he told her honestly.

"He's in New York. He sends me postcards."

Floored by that announcement, Marsh was at a loss for words. He hadn't had any idea that Lowell Graham kept in touch with his daughter. Two years ago he'd certainly been eager enough to relinquish all parental responsibility to Marsh.

"Can I go visit him in New York?" Cassie asked.

"Not by yourself," Jen said gently.

Cassie looked hopefully at Marsh.

"You know I'm around here all winter, short stuff."

Predictably, her gaze shifted to Linnea. "You could go with me. You know all about big cities too. We wouldn't have to worry about getting lost."

"Give her some time to think about it, Cass," Marsh cut in before Linnea could answer. He didn't think she was about to offer to escort Cassie, but he couldn't take any chances.

And then something occurred to him. Cassie treated Linnea like an older sister or another aunt. If Linnea had left, if she'd gone back to the city as she'd originally planned, he'd be willing to bet Cassie would be lobbying to go visit her right now instead of her father. Somehow Linnea had become family.

Confused, Marsh set that idea aside to consider later. He had been given a great deal of food for thought on this Thanksgiving Day, and all of it revolved around Linnea Bryan.

Linnea clearly saw Marsh's shifting emotions reflected on his face, and wryly decided none of them boded well for her. She searched her mind for a new topic of conversation, and promptly asked about the dogs.

"I didn't think you were all that fond of them," Marsh said challengingly.

"I've gotten used to them," she said, knowing she sounded testy herself. "They're sweet-natured. Not like the dogs I had experiences with before I came here."

"The ones who bit you?" Cassie asked.

"Those were the ones."

"Ones? Plural?" Marsh sounded surprised.

"Just lucky, I guess. The scars are all but invisible now, but when I was younger than Cassie I had two run-ins with unfriendly dogs. One was a pit bull, the other a Doberman."

"Knew a lot of folks who kept guard dogs?" he guessed.

"*Mother* knew lots of folks who did. Unfortunately, nobody thought to tell me that the nice puppies would eat me for breakfast if they were given half a chance."

Why she'd been so trusting the second time with the Doberman was beyond her, but maybe she'd been an optimist by nature even back then. She'd been incredibly lucky she hadn't been seriously hurt. And luckier still that she was able to conquer the fear of dogs she'd felt for so long.

She'd done it by immersing herself in the care and feeding of the Austins' Siberian huskies. When Marsh wasn't around, she often helped Cassie and Jen with their care. She knew them by name now, all thirty-five of them, and she'd begun thinking lately that she ought to hand Marsh a twenty-dollar bill and find out for herself if riding on a small sled through the snowy wilderness was as much fun as Jen claimed.

Marsh was staring at her with a speculative look on his face.

"What?" she asked.

"You're saying you don't have any more problems with our pooches?"

"None at all."

Despite her words, she couldn't quite hold his gaze. She looked down at her napkin, wadding it up in her hand. She hadn't exactly lied to Marsh. It was just that she did still flinch when the whole pack headed toward her at once. She wasn't about to admit that to him, of course, or tell him she sometimes found the dogs' resemblance to wolves a tad too pronounced for comfort.

She told herself it didn't matter if Marsh believed her or not. Why should she care? But that was a lie too. Even if he never changed his mind about their relationship, she did want his respect.

Defiant, she set aside the crumpled napkin and lifted her head. She looked him right in the eye. "Some people," she informed him, "are capable of changing. Some even embrace change."

TWELVE

The Dennison house had come alive in the last months. Now, in mid-December, with its brightly painted exterior festooned with Christmas decorations, winking colored lights, and wreaths at every door, it had left behind forever the designation "eyesore" and was in contention for the title "pride of the neighborhood."

"Gotta love what she's done," Jen said, whirring quietly up to Marsh's side as he stared out the bay window at Linnea's house.

Love thy neighbor, he thought.

That had never been his intention. He'd fought falling for her long and hard. And he'd thought he could get over her if only he set his mind to it.

Might as well face up to the truth. None of his attempts to protect his heart had worked. None would. He wanted Linnea to stay in Austin's Crossing.

He wanted to live with her, to be as permanent a part of her life as that house was.

He just hoped he hadn't waited too long to tell her he loved her. And that he could make her believe he did trust her to stick around for the long haul.

The biggest problem was that she barely spoke to him these days. The B&B kept her busy, but he suspected she was avoiding him too. He got most of his reports about what she was up to from Jen and Cassie, and some from Emma and other villagers. The numerous tourists whose business he and Linnea now shared filled in the remaining details. Did that mean she was hearing a great deal about him too? It was a good bet she was. In fact, he was counting on it.

A sharp jab to his upper arm brought his attention back to Aunt Jen. "Stop mooning after her and go do something. You can win her back if you set your mind to it."

"I wish I had your confidence." He rubbed the spot she'd poked, glad Jen wasn't *really* mad at him.

"Honestly! Men! You two were getting on in perfect harmony, until your lack of trust got in the way. She has no plans to leave. Neither do you. Why should you both be miserable apart when *you* can make a move that will set things right?"

Marsh shifted his attention back to the house next door, staring hard at Linnea's kitchen window, hoping for some glimpse of her through the glass. He knew Jen was right. More than that, he realized that the longer he delayed, the greater the danger that Linnea would simply give up on him, maybe even find someone else to love, someone else to marry. Some tourist, perhaps, a man who'd only be around part of the time.

Incensed by the thought of living next door and watching another man come home to her at night, Marsh abruptly understood how a forbidden obsession with a neighbor might come about. There was nothing forbidden about him loving Linnea, though, nothing standing between their future happiness except his stubborn pride.

His course of action was clear. Not easy, but simple and straightforward. He had to admit he'd been wrong. He had to tell Linnea he loved her. And he had to ask her to marry him and stay in Austin's Crossing forever. They could live in either house, whichever she preferred.

Frowning at his own image, reflected back at him by the glass in the bay window, Marsh conceded he had a lot to make up for. What was required was someplace private. A special place.

It didn't take him long to think of one. He knew the perfect spot.

"What's the schedule like this week?" he asked his aunt. "Any free stretches? I . . . need to make a test run with that new sled."

"Tomorrow afternoon." Jen's answer was prompt, but she sounded suspicious. "Do you want me to go along to add weight?"

"Thanks, but no." He inclined his head toward the house next door. "I have another passenger in mind."

"The most important thing to remember," Marsh told her, "is to hang on to the sled if it tips over."

Linnea nodded, but her thoughts weren't entirely on his crash course in dogsledding. She was still wondering why he'd invited her to make the three-mile cross-country trek he usually reserved for paying customers. Oh, she knew the official reason. He needed to test out a new lightweight sled and this was a day in midweek when he didn't have any rides scheduled. But they both knew Jen would have been delighted to go with him.

Was this some kind of test for her too? she wondered. For all she knew, Marsh still thought she was afraid of his dogs. Was this another attempt to prove to her that she was unsuited to be part of his life?

"Relax, Marsh," she said when he seemed inclined to lecture. There had never been any question but that she'd agree to go, whatever had motivated his invitation. "I've been wanting to ride 'in the basket' ever since the ground acquired its first blanket of snow."

He still looked worried. "Even for this short a trip, every passenger should know something about how things work. On longer trips I have everyone do just about everything, right down to cutting boughs for the dogs to sleep on at night."

Linnea knew he offered two longer outings, a day-long trip and a weekend excursion that blended cross-country skiing, dogsledding, and winter camping. On the eve of one of those, Jen had told her, he conducted a short course in survival training, which included the care and feeding of the dogs. Two women who'd stayed at Linnea's bed-and-breakfast for another night after one such trip had raved about the experience, even as they relished the comfort her place offered.

"Come here," Marsh ordered. "Put your left hand here, on the harness, then lift Tatupu slightly as you hook him to the sled."

Gamely, Linnea crunched toward the dogs through the packed snow, glad she'd worn lined boots and a warm snowmobile suit. The day was clear and so cold that each word appeared as a puff of frost in front of her face.

She gave Marsh a radiant smile. Whatever *his* intentions, she meant to enjoy this day to the fullest. She felt invigorated. Alive.

And for the first time in weeks, hopeful.

Tatupu was heavier than she'd expected. Each time she tried to fasten the hook, he hopped, taking the connection just out of reach. After several attempts, she looked to Marsh for help. "I feel like I'm trying to hang on to a kangaroo," she said in a rueful voice.

Marsh came in close, shadowing her arms with his, helping her tug on the linen-padded nylon webbing of the harness until Tatupu's front feet were off the ground. For a moment time seemed to stand still. Linnea ached to lean back against him, to turn in his arms and snuggle into his embrace.

Instead she stiffened her spine, and her resolve, and in a voice that was a trifle husky, said, "I think I've got it now."

The hookup was easy with both of them lifting.

"Try the next dog," Marsh instructed, stepping back.

She was both relieved and disappointed to be released from his embrace. It had been far too long since he'd held her. She wanted to turn and look at him, to judge for herself if she'd had any effect on him, but she didn't dare. She didn't want to risk disappointment.

Working with Fluffernutter was a trifle easier, but had its own challenges. The sweet-tempered Siberian wanted to lick Linnea's face. Wet tongue on such a cold day wasn't the most pleasant sensation. And the pooch had a bad case of doggy breath too.

Linnea worked her way through the team, hooking the dogs to the sled. Marsh went back to lecturing her about lead dogs and point dogs, who could replace a lead dog in an emergency, and wheel dogs, those that ran right in front of the sled. He was careful to avoid further physical contact.

When everything was ready and he'd checked and double-checked her attachments, he settled her into the basket with a minimum of fuss. He even managed to make sure she was tucked in and warm without ever touching her.

"What's in the zippered bag?" she asked, pointing to the brightly colored duffel-shaped object sharing the sled with her.

"Odds and ends. On long trips we carry extra booties for the dogs and sometimes even neoprene sweats to wrap their forelegs in during rest periods. If one of the dogs needs a longer rest than the others, he rides in the basket part of the way. Foolish likes to be zipped right into the bag."

She couldn't help smiling at that. Foolish was the spoiled brat of the family, and it wasn't just Cassie who coddled him.

Marsh pointed out the snow hook. "It's a sort of dry-land anchor, used to secure the sled if the driver has to stop to untangle lines." He cleared his throat and repeated his warning about hanging on to the sled if it should happen to tip over.

"Is that likely?" She was more curious than fearful. Now that she was actually sitting in the sled, she was eager for her adventure to begin. This low to the ground, she doubted she'd be hurt even if she did fall out.

"Likely, no. Possible, yes. We'll be taking a woodland trail, most of the time at around ten miles an hour. I want to run some tests, but even then our maximum speed won't be over twenty miles an hour. Still, it's always wise to be prepared."

"Motto of Boy Scouts and ex-cops," she muttered.

Ignoring the sarcasm, he went on. "We'll be underweight for this team, but I want to see how the sled handles, see if it would make a good sled for racing. I'd like to enter the Can-Am 250 next year."

She blinked in astonishment. "Two-fifty . . . as in miles?"

"Yes. It's part of a triple crown. The first race is a hundred and fifty miles, held in Ontario in January. The second is in northern Maine, at Fort Kent, and has a two-hundred-and-fifty-mile course. The third is four hundred miles. In Labrador. In March."

Linnea swiveled around, trying to see his face, to judge if he was serious. He looked it.

"I'm already practicing with twelve-dog teams, making eighteen-mile training runs."

Not your concern, she told herself as she settled into the sled again. But she had a feeling she'd worry anyway. Then an oddly logical explanation dawned on her, a reason for Marsh's sudden invitation to go out with him.

Maybe, just maybe, he hadn't given up on them. Was he taking her along today in the hope she'd come to love the sport as much as he did? And so she would worry less about his safety when he entered long-distance races? Once she'd experienced this for herself, she'd finally understand why it meant so much to him.

And maybe she was just foolishly playing the "what if" game again. Linnea tucked the blanket more tightly around her lower limbs and stared straight ahead. She was looking, she realized, at the back end of the dogs. Not the most inspiring view.

"Ready?" Marsh asked from behind and above as he stepped onto the back of the sled.

"Ready," she replied. She wondered if he was asking about more than this brief overland outing.

She told herself it didn't matter.

It was almost true, for within minutes, she'd forgotten everything but the exhilaration of the ride. Linnea loved her first experience with dogsled travel.

And when they were out of Austin's Crossing and in the woods, it just got better.

Evergreens closed in around them, shutting out the rest of the world. The silence was awe-inspiring, broken only by the sounds of paws crunching on the snow and birds twittering in the trees. And then Marsh began to sing softly, to his dogs and to her.

So far, so good, Marsh thought. He was almost at his usual stopping point, the halfway mark where he called a rest and took pictures of his customers.

He hadn't heard a peep out of Linnea, bundled up on the sled in front of him, except once when Zappa, one of the wheel dogs, had answered the call of nature on the run and she'd stifled a sound that he suspected was a laugh. From her vantage point, it had to have been a singularly aromatic moment.

Bongo, Gonzo, and Alf were running well, but Tatupu, for all his years of experience, seemed far too interested in their surroundings. Marsh was keeping a close eye on the dog. He'd noticed signs of moose and ruffled grouse along the trail, but other than the occasional chickadee, wildlife had stayed out of sight. He hoped that situation continued.

Still, the real focus of his attention was Linnea. She looked right at home in the sled, and he could sense the sheer delight she was taking in her surroundings. Her cherry-red snowmobile suit set off both a healthy complexion and her dark hair. She'd been letting it grow, he noticed, and dared hope that was because he'd once mentioned he liked longer hair on women.

No traces of the city girl he'd once thought she was were visible today. Marsh's spirits lifted at that observation. He was on the right track now. He was sure of it. When they finally stopped, they'd have lots of privacy. Miles from civilization, they'd be able to work out a plan for their future without interruption.

He didn't kid himself that it would be easy, even if she fell into his arms and agreed with everything he suggested. She'd already come far. She'd started out terrified of the dogs. But there was only so much adapting a person could do.

Unable to alter the direction of his thoughts, Marsh's logic took him to a place he did not want to go. All the old doubts crowded into his mind. He knew for a fact that love couldn't overcome every obstacle.

Anita had said she'd loved him, until he'd asked her to live with him in rural Maine and raise sled dogs and children. Linnea had said she loved him. But that was before he'd deliberately set out to drive her away. He—

It happened so quickly, even Marsh's experience, combined with rapid reflexes, wasn't sufficient to prevent an accident.

Tatupu caught sight of a rabbit. His sudden attempt to chase it overwhelmed the lightweight sled and passenger and promptly threw the entire team into chaos. The confusion was compounded when Fluffernutter collided with a stretch of fence, half-hidden by the snow. Then Gonzo briefly came in contact with the sharp barbed wire. His howls of pain created even greater pandemonium.

"Hang on!" Marsh yelled as the sled tipped perilously to one side.

The team continued to pull it forward, but now they'd left the trail and hazards loomed up on either side. Tree limbs and low-growing bushes presented almost as much danger as the remnants of that hidden fence.

Seconds later they stopped.

Marsh threw out the ground anchor and hopped off the back of the sled, calling softly to the dogs to calm them. Linnea was already scrambling out of the basket on her own, adequate proof that she was unhurt.

In spite of the fact that she'd twice been bitten by dogs, she didn't hesitate to wade into the middle of the milling canines to help him free Fluffernutter and Gonzo. Ignoring their initial snarls, she crooned the same song he'd been singing earlier, soothing them so he could take a close look at the scrapes and cuts the two dogs had sustained.

"Not too bad," he said a minute later. "Minor damage only."

"You're certain? If they're injured, they can ride in the sled on the way back."

"I'm certain."

And at last he was also certain about something else. He'd been altogether wrong about Linnea Bryan.

She did belong here.

With him.

Forever.

Linnea's heart rate slowly settled, now that the danger was past. For the first time she took a good look at their surroundings and realized that if she were out here alone, she would be completely lost. She'd have no inkling of how to get back to Austin's Crossing. She'd probably freeze to death if she tried, be nothing but an icicle by the side of the trail.

But she wasn't alone.

She had Marsh.

She could feel his gaze boring into her. With a strange hesitance, she stood up, turned, and faced him. Then her eyes widened in alarm at the sight of blood on his face. "You're hurt!"

His hand went to his chin. His fingers came away stained with red, but he shrugged it off. "Just a scratch."

Then he narrowed his eyes to peer more closely at her. "You didn't come out of this unscathed, either."

She looked down at herself, at her hands, and saw no sign of injury. She was pretty sure he wasn't referring to the bruise she could feel coming up on her hip. That was definitely out of sight. "Where?"

Instead of answering, he closed the distance between them and lifted the hand still marked with his blood to touch her cheek. "Matching flaws," he murmured.

"We already had those."

"How so?"

"Well, maybe not physical flaws. Faults, though. We've plenty of them in common. Maybe it goes back to the ancestor we share. Stubbornness. Determination. Loyalty. We match on all those."

Love was the only "fault" she still wasn't sure about. Did they share the strength of that as well?

"Guess there's only one way to handle all those faults," he said, "only one solution for dealing with them."

"Oh?"

"Sometimes," he said, stroking her cheek once more with a gentleness that made her melt inside, "if you combine faults, you can turn them into virtues. I think we've just proved we make a pretty good team. An unbeatable team."

Did she dare hope? "Are you suggesting we combine my business and yours?"

"I'm suggesting we combine my life and yours. I want you to stay, to marry me, to be not only a role model but a mother to Cassie."

Breathing suddenly took tremendous effort. Linnea wanted to shout yes and throw herself into his arms. She managed to hold back. There was a lot riding on this decision—their whole future. She had to be certain it wasn't just the adrenaline rush from their narrow escape that was making Marsh talk this way.

"That's a lot to ask," she said cautiously. "And you weren't so sure I fit the job description for role model just a few weeks ago."

"I was an idiot."

He bent his head, clearly intent upon kissing her, but she pulled back. "I won't be able to think if you do that."

Reluctantly, he gave her space, but not much. He was standing very close, one hand on her shoulder, the other still touching her scratched face.

"You were right about changes," he admitted.

She had to fight back a smile. "You say that with all the enthusiasm of a man having a tooth pulled."

"Give me a break here, Linnea. I'm trying to apologize to you."

"I know. And I know that even a month ago I'd never have won that concession from you. You were dead set against any change."

"Changes aren't all bad," he said, and with that a dam seemed to break. He went on to list all the reasons why she should accept his proposal. One was missing, though, and it was the only one that carried any weight with her.

Tatupu whined and nuzzled her hand. She stroked him idly, watching Marsh's eyes. She knew the exact moment when he realized what he'd neglected to mention.

A sheepish smile tilted one corner of his mouth. "You're going to make me say it, aren't you?"

"Is it that hard?"

The smile turned into a full-fledged grin. "It's the easiest thing in the world, Linnea."

He got down on one knee in the snow in front of her, ignoring the playful bump Tatupu gave his shoulder. "I love you, Linnea Bryan. Will you marry me and live with me and raise children and sled dogs together for as long as we both shall live?"

"Oh, yes," she said.

One of the dogs hit her from behind, its weight driving her into Marsh's embrace and sending them both tumbling to the ground in a tangle of arms and legs. This time she felt no fear and had no wish at all to squirm and break free.

Laughing together, they kissed to put a seal on their love. Neither of them would have noticed just then if the dogs had taken the sled and gone on home without them.

THE EDITORS' CORNER

Spring is just around the bend, and we have four new LOVESWEPTs guaranteed to warm your heart with thoughts of love and romance. Make a new set of friends by reading these touching stories of love discovered, love denied, and love reborn, included in our March lineup. So sit back, relax, grab a LOVESWEPT, and help us usher in a new season of love!

Karen Leabo's *Brides of Destiny* series continues with **LANA'S LAWMAN**, LOVESWEPT #826. Lana Gaston finds she can no longer deny a fortune-teller's prediction when Sloan Bennett appears out of the thunderstorm like a knight in shining armor. She's never forgotten how it feels to lose herself in Sloan's embrace and his steamy kisses. But can a single mom surrender her hard-earned independence long enough to find her future in a street cop's soul?

Karen Leabo maps the territory of true yearning and its power to heal old sorrows in this tale of heartfelt passion and dreams that will never die.

Danger and desire make for a perilous and seductive combination in Janis Reams Hudson's **ONE RAINY NIGHT**, LOVESWEPT #827. Moments after Zane Houston opens his door, shots ring out and he tackles his pretty neighbor, Becca Cameron. Becca is shocked by her reaction to this hard stranger, and when more violence sends them running for cover, attraction gives way to white-hot need. He makes her feel brave and sexy, driving her down a reckless road; but if they survive the ride, will they dare admit it's love? Janis Reams Hudson entangles a desperate ex-cop and a spirited pixie in this story of heartstopping suspense and irresistible passion.

Max Hogan makes a living looking for trouble, but ever since his wife, Grace, sent him packing, he's vowed to find a way back into her life in **EX AND FOREVER**, LOVESWEPT #828, by Linda Warren. Grace insists that she won't be wooed or won over, but when they join forces to catch a clever con man, sparks explode and nothing will put out the flames. He promised her his love for a lifetime. Can Grace convince Max that forever would be even better? Linda Warren's latest story of a couple searching for a second chance is both deliciously sexy and irresistibly funny all at once!

Speaking of second chances, newcomer Stephanie Bancroft weaves a tale of shattering emotion and desperate yearning in **ALMOST A FAMILY**, LOVESWEPT #829. Virginia Catron and Bailey Kallihan had shared the worst that could happen—the loss of their son. Now the child is again theirs to raise. Virginia has struggled past her grief to build a new life, but would rebuilding a family with Bailey mean losing her heart all over again? Stephanie Bancroft poignantly reminds us of how forgiveness can rekindle lost love in this novel of stolen innocence and the power of hope.

Happy reading!

With warmest wishes,

Shauna Summers

Joy Abella

Shauna Summers   Joy Abella
Editor   Administrative Editor

P.S. Watch for these Bantam women's fiction titles coming in March. *New York Times* bestseller Iris Johansen is back with another heartstopping tale of suspense and intrigue. In **LONG AFTER MIDNIGHT**, gifted research scientist Kate Denham mistakenly believes she's finally carved out a secure life for herself and her son, until she is suddenly thrown into a nightmare world where danger is all around and trusting a handsome stranger is the only way to survive. From national bestseller Patricia Potter comes **THE SCOTSMAN WORE SPURS**, a thrilling tale of danger and romance as a Scottish peer and a woman with a mission meet in the unlikeliest place—a cattle drive. And immediately following this page, preview the Bantam women's fiction titles on sale *now*!

For current information on Bantam's women's fiction, visit our new web site, *Isn't It Romantic,* at the following address: **http://www.bdd.com/romance**

Don't miss these extraordinary books
by your favorite Bantam authors

On sale in January:

GUILTY AS SIN
by Tami Hoag

THE DIAMOND SLIPPER
by Jane Feather

STOLEN HEARTS
by Michelle Martin

GUILTY AS SIN

BY

TAMI HOAG

Don't miss the *New York Times* hardcover bestseller soon to be available in paperback.

The kidnapping of eight-year-old Josh Kirkwood irrevocably altered the small town of Deer Lake, Minnesota. Even after the arrest of a suspect, fear maintains its grip, and questions of innocence and guilt linger. Now, as prosecutor Ellen North prepares to try her toughest case yet, she faces not only a sensation-driven press corps, political maneuvering, and her ex-lover as attorney for the defense, but an unwanted partner: Jay Butler Brooks, bestselling true-crime author and media darling, has been granted total access to the case—and to her. All the while, someone is following Ellen with deadly intent. When a second child is kidnapped while her prime suspect sits in jail, Ellen realizes that the game isn't over, it has just begun again. . . .

"If I were after you for nefarious purposes," he said as he advanced on Ellen, "would I be so careless as to approach you here?"

He pulled a gloved hand from his pocket and gestured gracefully to the parking lot, like a magician drawing attention to his stage.

"If I wanted to harm you," he said, stepping closer, "I would be smart enough to follow you home, find a way to slip into your house or garage, catch you where there would be little chance of witnesses or interference." He let those images take firm root in her mind. "That's what I would do if I were the sort of rascal who preys on women." He smiled again. "Which I am not."

"Who *are* you and what *do* you want?" Ellen demanded, unnerved by the fact that a part of her brain catalogued his manner as charming. No, not charming. Seductive. Disturbing.

"Jay Butler Brooks. I'm a writer—true crime. I can show you my driver's license if you'd like," he offered, but made no move to reach for it, only took another step toward her, never letting her get enough distance between them to diffuse the electric quality of the tension.

"I'd like for you to back off," Ellen said. She started to hold up a hand, a gesture meant to stop him in his tracks—or a foolish invitation for him to grab hold of her arm. Pulling the gesture back, she hefted her briefcase in her right hand, weighing its potential as a weapon or a shield. "If you think I'm getting close enough to you to look at a DMV photo, you must be out of your mind."

"Well, I have been so accused once or twice, but it never did stick. Now my Uncle Hooter, he's a different story. I could tell you some tales about him. Over dinner, perhaps?"

"Perhaps not."

He gave her a crestfallen look that was ruined by the sense that he was more amused than affronted. "After I waited for you out here in the cold?"

"After you stalked me and skulked around in the shadows?" she corrected him, moving another step backward. "After you've done your best to frighten me?"

"I frighten you, Ms. North? You don't strike me as the sort of woman who would be easily frightened. That's certainly not the impression you gave at the press conference."

"I thought you said you aren't a reporter."

"No one at the courthouse ever asked," he confessed. "They assumed the same way you assumed. Forgive my pointing it out at this particular moment, but assumptions can be very dangerous things. Your boss needs to have a word with someone about security. This is a highly volatile case you've got here. Anything might happen. The possibilities are virtually endless. I'd be happy to discuss them with you. Over drinks," he suggested. "You look like you could do with one."

"If you want to see me, call my office."

"Oh, I want to see you, Ms. North," he murmured, his voice an almost tangible caress. "I'm not big on appointments, though. Preparation time eliminates spontaneity."

"That's the whole point."

"I prefer to catch people . . . off balance," He admitted. "They reveal more of their true selves."

"I have no intention of revealing anything to you." She stopped her retreat as a group of people emerged from the main doors of City Center. "I should have you arrested."

He arched a brow. "On what charge, Ms. North? Attempting to hold a conversation? Surely y'all are not so inhospitable as your weather here in Minnesota, are you?"

She gave him no answer. The voices of the people who had come out of the building rose and fell, only the odd word breaking clear as they made their way down the sidewalk. She turned and fell into step with the others as they passed.

Jay watched her walk away, head up, chin out, once again projecting an image of cool control. She didn't like being caught off guard. He would have bet money she was a list maker, a rule follower, the kind of woman who dotted all her *i*'s and crossed all her *t*'s, then double-checked them for good measure. She liked boundaries. She like control. She had no intention of revealing anything to him.

"But you already have, Ms. Ellen North," he said, hunching up his shoulders as the wind bit a little harder and spat a sweep of fine white snow across the parking lot. "You already have."

THE DIAMOND SLIPPER

BY

JANE FEATHER

What comes to mind when you think of a diamond slipper? Cinderella, perhaps?

That's what Cordelia Brandenburg imagines when her godparents arrange a marriage for her with a man she's never met—a marriage that will take her to Versailles, far from her childhood home. The betrothal gift is a charm bracelet with a tiny diamond slipper attached . . . as befits a journey into a fairy-tale future. But when her escort to the wedding is the sensual, teasing Viscount Leo Kierston, it's love at first sight for the young, headstrong Cordelia. And while Leo sees only a spoiled child, Cordelia is determined to show him the woman underneath. But there is no escaping her arranged marriage, and she's devastated to discover that her husband is a loathsome tyrant who will stop at nothing to satisfy his twisted desires. But he also has a terrible secret . . . a secret that will bring a long-awaited chance for revenge, the dark threat of danger, and the freedom of a vibrant passion.

"Which hand do you choose, my lord?"

It seemed that short of bodily removing her, he was destined to play chess with her. Harmless enough, surely? Resigned, he tapped her closed right hand.

"You drew black!" she declared with a note of triumph that he recognized from the afternoon's dicing. "That means I have the first move." She turned the chess table so that the white pieces were in front of her and moved pawn to king four. Then sat back, regarding him expectantly.

"Unusual move," he commented ironically, playing the countermove.

"I like to play safe openings," she confided, bringing out her queen's pawn. "Then when the board opens up, I can become unconventional."

"Good God! You mean there's one activity you actually choose to play by the book! You astound me, Cordelia!"

Cordelia merely grinned and brought out her queen's knight in response to his pawn challenge.

They played in silence and Leo was sufficiently absorbed in the game to be able to close his mind to her scantily clad presence across from him. She played a good game but he had the edge, mainly because she took risks with a degree of abandon.

Cordelia frowned over the board, chewing her bottom lip. Her last gamble had been a mistake and she could see serious danger in the next several moves if she didn't move her queen out of harm's way. If only she could intercept with a pawn, but none of her pawns were in the proper position, unless . . .

"What was that noise?"

"What noise?" Leo looked up, startled at the sound of her voice breaking the long silence.

"Over there. In the corner. A sort of scrabbling." She gestured to the far corner of the room. Leo turned to look. When he looked back at the board, her pawn had been neatly diverted and now protected her queen.

Leo didn't notice immediately. "Probably a mouse," he said. "The woodwork's alive with them."

"I hope it's not a rat," she said with an exaggerated shiver and conspicuously united her rooks. "Let's see if that will help."

It was Leo's turn to frown now. Something had changed on the board in front of him. It didn't look the way he remembered it, but he couldn't see . . . and then he did.

Slowly, he reached out and picked up the deviated pawn. He raised his eyes and looked across at her. Cordelia was flushing, so transparently guilty he wanted to laugh again.

"If you must cheat, why don't you do it properly," he said conversationally, returning the pawn to its original position. "You insult my intelligence to imagine that I wouldn't notice. Do you think I'm blind?"

Cordelia shook her head, her cheeks still pink. "It's not really possible to cheat at chess, but I do so hate to lose. I can't seem to help it."

"Well, I have news for you. You are going to learn to help it." He replaced her rooks in their previous position. "We are going to play this game to the bitter end and you are going to lose it. It's your move, and as I see it, you can't help but sacrifice your queen."

Cordelia stared furiously at the pieces. She couldn't bring herself to make the only move she had, the one that would mean surrendering her queen. Without it she would be helpless; besides it was a symbolic piece. She would be acknowledging she'd lost once she gave it up. "Oh, very well," she said crossly. "I suppose you win. There's no need to play further."

Leo shook his head. He could read her thoughts

as if they were written in black ink. Cordelia was the worst kind of loser. She couldn't bear to play to a loss. "There's every need. Now make your move."

Her hand moved to take the queen and then she withdrew it. "But there's no point."

"The point, my dear Cordelia, is that you are going to play this game to its conclusion. Right up to the moment when you topple your king and acknowledge defeat. Now *move.*"

"Oh, very well." She shot out her hand, half rising on her stool, leaning over the board as if it took her whole body to move the small wooden carving. Her knees caught the edge of the table, toppling it, and the entire game disintegrated, half the pieces tumbling to the carpet. "Oh, what a nuisance!" Hastily, she steadied the rocking table.

"Why, of all the graceless, brattish, mean-spirited things to do!" Leo, furious, leaped up. Leaning over the destroyed board, he grabbed her shoulders, half shaking, half hauling her toward him.

"But I didn't to it on purpose!" Cordelia exclaimed. "Indeed, I didn't. It was an accident."

"You expect me to believe that?" He jerked her hard toward him, unsure what he intended doing with her but for the moment lost in disappointed anger that she could do something so malicious and childish. He moved his grip to her upper arms, half lifting her over the board, Cordelia's protestations of innocence growing ever more vociferous.

Then matters became very confused. He was shaking her, she was yelling, his mouth was on hers. Her yells ceased. His hands were hard on her arms and her body was pressed against his. . . .

From the fresh, new voice of

MICHELLE MARTIN

comes a sparkling romance
in the bestselling tradition of
Jayne Ann Krentz

STOLEN HEARTS

An ex–jewel thief pulls the con of her life, but one
man is determined to catch her—and never
let her get away.

*For Tess Alcott, chocolate was a vice, stealing jewels was
pure pleasure. So when her ruthless former "employer"
turned up to coerce her into taking part in a daring heist,
he didn't have to twist her arm too far. He only had to hold
out the lure of the magnificent Farleigh emeralds. To win
them, all Tess needs to do is convince one sweet old lady and
one grouchy, blue-blooded—and distractingly handsome—
lawyer that she's the missing heiress to a fortune. But Tess
doesn't realize the danger, until the infuriating lawyer
beats her at her own game and steals her most prized
possession . . . her heart. Now Tess doesn't know which
she wants more: the gorgeous emeralds or the gorgeous
emerald-eyed lawyer. . . .*

She padded down the back stairs in her bare feet, to
avoid Jane and Luke, and walked into the library.
Luke stood at the river-rock fireplace, a snifter of

brandy balanced in his long fingers. He stared into it as if seeking the answers to the universe.

"Oops! Sorry," she said, striding briskly into the room as if her very being was not centered on the green-eyed monster from hell. "I didn't mean to disturb you. I just came for a book. Something like Richardson's *Pamela*. Guaranteed to knock you out cold inside of two minutes."

"You're looking for *Pamela*?" he said, his hands still wrapped around the brandy snifter. "You nearly fell asleep over your cup of after-dinner hot chocolate."

She walked toward the bookshelves, hoping to find a book and escape quickly. "Hodgkins laced the hot chocolate with caffeine," she said calmly. "I'm convinced of it."

"His dislike of heartless cons exceeds even my own. But then, he's known Jane longer."

"Fortunately," Tess said lightly, "Jane relies on her own opinion, not on that of her butler or watchdog, I mean lawyer."

"This *watchdog* will protect Jane from your machinations with the last breath in his body."

"I expected nothing less," Tess said, scanning the shelves for *Pamela*.

"Who are you really, Tess Alcott?"

"You got me. I'll let you know when I find out."

"So you intend to play this amnesia story for all it's worth?"

Rage erupted in Tess and spun her around to face her enemy. "Do you remember your fifth-birthday party?" she demanded.

Luke looked surprised at suddenly being under attack. "Sure."

"Do you remember what your childhood bedroom looked like?"

"Of course."

"Do you remember what your favorite food was?"

"Yes."

"Well, I don't!" Tess said bitterly. "You're supposed to be such a hotshot lawyer, Mansfield, but you're batting less than a hundred when it comes to knowing what the truth is about me!"

She spun back to the bookshelves, trying to get her temper and her pain under control. The library was silent for what seemed a very long moment.

"I'm beginning to think you're right," Luke said gently. "But still, even with my lousy batting average, you can't win."

"There's that male arrogance rearing its ugly head again," Tess said, standing on tiptoe to read the titles on the upper shelves, wanting to relax into Luke's quiet but not daring to. "But in a way you're right, Mansfield. I can't really win because I don't have anything to lose. I'm looking for my past, remember? If Jane isn't there, it's no skin off my nose. I'll eventually find someone who was there and I'll be able to conduct my own little 'Up Close and Personal' interview. So yap away, Mansfield, you can only give yourself a sore throat."

His chuckle rumbled up and down her spine. Without looking, she knew that Luke had leaned his back against the fireplace mantel and was studying her from head to toe.

"Love your negligee," he said.

Tess forced herself to laugh as she grabbed *Pamela* and turned to him. The brandy snifter was resting on the mantel. His hands were free. He seemed more dangerous that way. "I think it's best to choose function over form," she said a little breathlessly, tension coiling within her. "In my line of work, it's often necessary to make a quick, and unscheduled, exit and that means no time to grab your clothes if you're sleeping in the nude . . . as I found out the hard way in my youth."

Luke's grin broadened, lightening his face, eroding the cynical mask. "Now that is something I dearly would have loved to see."

"Six French *gendarmes* had the dubious pleasure instead," Tess said, walking back across the room. It seemed to stretch on for miles before her. "Fortunately, the shock of seeing a naked girl running across the rooftops of the Left Bank kept them from firing their guns and I was able to make my getaway unscathed. Later I heard about an American bank robber who pulled all of his jobs in the nude because, I am told on the greatest authority, if you've only seen someone naked, you can't recognize them dressed."

"That wouldn't work where you're concerned," Luke murmured, his gaze forcing her to a stop directly in front of him. "It's a good thing you didn't meet those *gendarmes* the next day."

A blush flooded Tess's cheeks. "Why, Mr. Mansfield, I do believe you're actually paying me a compliment."

"It has been known to happen," Luke said, sounding a bit surprised himself. "I once made some very nice remarks about a racing skiff I was assigned at Harvard."

"Careful, Mansfield. Such unbridled enthusiasm will have you running amok."

"Running amok sounds wonderful just now," Luke said with a sigh, his hand reaching out and brushing against her cheek, lingering there, stilling her breath.

The world tilted crazily beneath Tess's feet as he slowly lowered his head to hers. "Luke," she whispered, and had no idea what to say next.

His lips met hers in a gentle joining of warmth against warmth. Hunger broke free within her. She wrapped her arms around his neck, standing on tiptoe to press herself against him, her mouth deepening the kiss of its own accord. With a groan, Luke slid his arms around her, holding her tight, his sensual mouth moving hungrily over hers.

It was good, so good. It was the closest thing to heaven Tess had ever known.

And it ended in the next moment, as sanity abruptly returned.

She jerked away, her book clutched to her chest, the back of one hand pressed against her mouth. "What the *hell* do you think you're doing?" she hissed.

His breath as ragged as her own, Luke stared down at her. Then anger blazed in his eyes. "The same might be asked of you, *Elizabeth*," he said. "Just how far were you willing to go to win me over to your side?"

Something in Tess, newly born, died in that moment. Oh God, he had been using her, testing her. And she had fallen for it. For a moment her hand itched to strike the superiority from Luke's handsome face. Instead, she gripped her book even harder.

"Don't think you can use your masculine charms to seduce me out of this house," she snapped. "I am neither that stupid nor that desperate!"

She stalked from the room, slamming the library door shut behind her.

On sale in February:

LONG AFTER MIDNIGHT
by Iris Johansen

SPRING COLLECTION
by Judith Krantz

THE SCOTSMAN WORE SPURS
by Patricia Potter